D R A C U L A,

The Reemergence of Vlad!

A novel and screenplay

By

Richard Reich

TABLE OF CONTENTS:

PART I   THE REEMERGENCE   P. 5

PART II   DRACULA ... REVISITED   P. 41

PART III   THE YOUNG VAMPIRES   P. 95

PART IV   THE COMMUNION   P. 131

PART V   ARMAGEDDON   P. 179

DRACULA,

The Reemergence of Vlad!

The scene is set at the home of Count Dracula, evil incarnate, immortal corrupter, destroyer of life and pilferer of souls. We find him preoccupied as he attends to one of the problems that occasionally plagues his unholy existence... Namely, he's been out too late and lightly burned by the rays of the early morning sun.

Dracula - Damn, that smarts. Lightly burned hell. That's a searing burn if ever there was one. For a body that could be considered dead for all practical purposes, it sure knows when there is pain to be felt. Another ten minutes and I would have been Kentucky Fried Extra Crispy...

Renfield - (Renfield comes to the door while Dracula waits in the alcove.) What was that Master?

Dracula - I said, another ten minutes and I would have been Colonel Sanders Rotisserie Gold, with a side order of fries. Well at least I wasn't blinded. I'll regenerate my skin soon enough but there's nothing worse than being burned and blinded at the same time.

Renfield - You're forgetting the stake through the heart. Surely that must be the worst.

Dracula - I'm certainly not looking forward to that. Listen Renfield, you know that topic makes me edgy. I'm already burned as it is.

Renfield - Maybe you should get a job closer to home. You might like a night watchman position at the hospital, especially in front of the emergency ward. You could see a lot of bloody bodies there as they're brought in. (Dracula walks through the entrance, takes off cape.) Some would have broken bones with neatly severed arteries still pulsating with spurting blood. (Dracula's eyes glaze over as he licks his lips.) There may even be corpses, freshly dead with only a subtle hint of rot. (Dracula snaps out of his trance.)

Dracula - Sounds like you've been reading those gourmet cookbooks, Renfield. But, you know only a living victim is fresh enough. You're letting your own putrid tastes influence you again.

Renfield - Sorry master.

Dracula - That does sound nice though, doesn't it... a nice change from stalking down at the boatyard, having to depend on wharf waifs and drunken sots for what little sustenance they offer. Spurting blood you say?

Renfield - Yes.

Dracula - You're beginning to think like a vampire, Renfield. Are you sure you've never been bitten?

Renfield - No master, or you might try to be an operating room attendant, where you could watch the surgeon use all sorts of sharp instruments to make the victims' blood flow, they call them patients... Why a victim of a major organ operation might lose a gallon or more. Of course, it might put quite a strain on your self-control. Do you think you could restrain yourself at the sight of so much...

Dracula - Don't bore me with your feeble attempt at dramatics. You know the essence of vampirism is the consummate ability to exercise control until the last possible moment, when ahhh ... (fantasizing with eyes closed), teeth sink deeply into soft warm flesh tapping into a rushing supply of lovely life-sustaining blood (his lips start quivering). How can you even talk of restraint, you worm eating idiot? If you had even an ounce of control you'd never contemplate eating such disgusting creatures.

Renfield - Please don't master. It's only bugs. I only like the bugs and sometimes small animals, birds especially. I like to fish for birds with worms sometimes... but worms have barely any life to them, except when they get trapped in a water puddle... then I just like to watch them.

Dracula - Worms, slugs, bugs, Renfield your vulgarity can actually amaze me at times. You know Renfield, I doubt you could ever attain vampire status, one of the rare cases where the bite would have no effect.

Renfield - I'm sorry, master.

Dracula - No matter, you serve me and are rewarded. Are you not?

Renfield - Yes master. Your coffin is ready.

Dracula - Good Renfield, you may tend to your pursuits, but stay out of trouble. (Renfield giggles and scuttles off.)

1

Dracula retires to a chamber in the basement where a heavy oaken casket is kept. He deftly slides back the lid and settles into a depression worn into the ancient earth. As he moves the lid into position he hears cricket noises and pauses to utter an anathema against Renfield and his penchant for collecting, storing and later devouring insects. The next evening Dracula stirs from his moribund state, arises and repairs to the kitchen where he finds Renfield busily preparing a large cooking pot for the stove.

Dracula - Ah Renfield, have you sufficiently depleted the members of class Insecta for your unbridled dining pleasure?

Renfield - Please master, you embarrass me. I'm preparing the usual assortment of mealworms, beetles and centipedes. I did come across a nice treat though, a nest of baby moles. It almost looks as though they have eyes that could open if they were not doomed to blindness all their lives. Do you think they might learn to see if they were forced to live above the ground?

Dracula - I don't know, but I don't want them scratching around or squeaking downstairs with your damned crickets. I won't have it. They're not as nocturnal as you think and they're just a damn nuisance.

Renfield - Yes master.

Dracula - Are you using some Cajun herbs? Reminds me a bit of New

The Reemergence of Vlad!

Orleans. You can't beat a good Mardi Gras festival for an easy bite on the neck.

Renfield - Yes, it's sort of a Cajun-style gumbo. Mealworms are very good for gumbo.

Dracula - Gumbo, gumbo! I have teeth as sharp as the finest surgeon's blade and you talk of gumbo. I think I need some country air. All this talk of heart stakes, gumbo, meal worms, crickets... I tell you Renfield, I need a vacation from this dull harbor town. How long have we been here anyway?

Renfield - Ten years master.

Dracula - Yes, ten years of the same iron poor blood, drunken dullards, bar maids, even the dance show girls don't excite me. Used to be I could enjoy tearing them away from their wholesome happy little lives, watching them slowly weaken and turn away from their dearest friends and family. First in despair, then with soul rending devotion only to me, the master of their eternal immortal damnation. Nowadays it's a rare find to encounter even the youngest waifs who haven't already had their minds warped by the strongest addicting substance from the orient or even actual brain damage. I swear Renfield sometimes these young girls, the ones with the black leather fashions particularly, think that a pierced neck vein is simply the next logical fashion statement after piercing their ears and nose. Why do you realize that if vampirism becomes some kind of cheapened hyped-up fad like shaving your head or tattooing a breast, it'll lose that luster or veneer of evil that only genuine horror can evoke!

Renfield - Wouldn't it be thrilling though master, to see how the body counts of the ones you've maimed or done in might compare with the other popular cruelties of the day... like that AIDS disease or accidental death by dismemberment. You could have all those pretty news ladies talking about you on their TV programs. Wouldn't you love to hear Connie Chung and Lynne Russell repeating your name over and over? We could invite them over and I'd serve a nice meal worm casserole.

Dracula - (snaps to attention after staring vacantly) That might be amusing at that, you worm toothed bug baster. You know it's a subject I've contemplated often down through the centuries and sometimes because I've had to. Similar to many cults such as witchery, black magic and the like, the essence of the vampire is the cloak of darkness, the barrier of the night, the unwary unsuspecting victim, completely innocent of and naive to his situation until of course it is too late. And it's almost always too late. That's why you don't see cases of anemic neck bitten teenagers or drunken sots turning up in medical journals with their wounds and symptoms for the world to see. They don't even remember what has happened. And of course after the coup de grace, the death bite, while the body may have all the appearances of death and may in fact be dead, because not all who are bitten become vampires, the neck wounds are rapidly healing owing to the intermingling with immortal blood there.

Renfield - Master, I'm sure you could give Connie Chung goose bumps. It would be a top ranking story undoubtedly. There might be mass hysteria, even copy-cat blood sucking. Wouldn't that be shocking, and all in your name, of course!

Dracula - Yes copy-cat vampires might throw them off the scent a bit. It would be very difficult though for a real vampire to let himself be known publicly. It goes against our nature, the survival and protective sense is too strong. In fact our only real weakness is the loss of anonymity from those with the intelligence to fear us.

Renfield - And when they come with the stake for pounding right through...

Dracula - Enough, isn't your gumbo ready yet? You must be hungry, eat Renfield.

Renfield - Thank you master.

Dracula - I might play with the media from time to time but to risk direct publicity... too many people wouldn't hesitate to test our weaknesses in every possible way. I know these Americans. All you have to do is read these Hollywood tabloids to see they can be more ruthless than the meanest wolfhound when they go after a big story.

Renfield - We could always escape again if we had to... Remember the time they caught you biting a grandmother in a movie-house when the lights came up and you didn't notice the picture had ended! They got a good look at you. The police even made sketches but we got away, didn't we?

Dracula - Yes, Renfield... Maybe it's time we journeyed once more. I suppose I probably could tempt fate a little in the meantime then, why not? It's been hundreds of years since I've been really worried about myself.

Renfield - How about that time master... when you were sure you wanted to marry and then you brought your lovely young bride to be home for the evening but she couldn't get used to sleeping during the daytime? She left you to find another even though she had already been bitten.

Dracula - I remember well, a hot blooded Italian. She was also a singer, as well as a beauty. Did you know Renfield? She could have sung her wonderful songs for me forever. Her strict Catholic upbringing caused her to have a strong aversion to sleeping in an earth filled coffin by day. Most unfortunate. Yes she was quite unlike many people who take their religion as a chore on the week's schedule, or a second-natured hobby. A lot of people don't realize that the sects of Christianity and other main religions had certain ancient origins, most attributed to the ramblings of that Jesus character whom they believed possessed the powers of the undead. These early people organized religions in order to overcome their fear of the Dracula clan and the influence of vampires. They wanted, or rather had to believe there was someone, some immortal even more powerful than the vampire who could also bring them eternal life and who could put them in the most wonderful place... what they call heaven. You see these religious planners had to upstage us, had to do us one better. So they created their fantasy ideas to fight their fear of one day, or night more likely, becoming a true undead with no other law but self-preservation and the craving for blood.

Renfield - If these religions are fantasy then why have they become so popular while you can only claim Hollywood movies... Some of them, even you must admit master, sometimes seem more funny when they try to be serious and vice versa. Excuse me, master.

Dracula - That is the irony, isn't it, Renfield? That these whimsical beliefs about Bible stories and their Sunday meditations have exploded in popularity over the ages while the Dracula family endures the humiliation of merely an occasional set of fangs or mask as tribute at Halloween time. Ah those kids can be cute though, it almost kills you. I like to wonder on occasion what it might have been like if vampirism had been given the same hype and promotion as Christianity. And what if the church leaders were hunted down to have stakes rammed in their hearts as was commonly the habit with vampires in the early days. Maybe if we had thought to choose a special day of the week or published our book first, the roles of religion and vampires might have been reversed, eh Renfield?

Renfield - We could talk to people and they wouldn't cringe, right master? Would we be wealthy like Jimmy Swagger and Pats Roberton? You might buy a nice waterproof coffin, while I could send for insects by mail order. That would be nice, ever so.

Dracula - You would think that after all these centuries I would have higher aspirations than living in a dank cellar of a creaky old house. Well, I do Renfield and one day I shall tell you about them. However, at the moment I have more immediate concerns. I feel an evening of entertainment is in order. Maybe I'll fly over to Palm Springs. They're starting to film a new movie with a young starlet I'd very much like to meet.

Renfield - Be careful master. I hope you'll invite her for a stay. I'm sure that I would like her. You know I don't see the movies very often. Ever since the manager caught me eating buttered beetles instead of popcorn.

Dracula has already left leaving a brooding Renfield to await his return.

2

Dracula lands on the set of Buffy the Vampire Slayer, Part Three - The Bubble Bath of Blood. He notices a group of extras dressed up in party costumes and joins the group.

Dracula - (thinking to himself) There really are quite a few starlets I'd like to meet. Madonna would probably make an excellent Countess. The way she enjoys putting those celebrity boyfriends of hers into fits of rage is perfectly evil and delightful. But she's always wearing those big crosses like that fetching young comic talent, Christina Applegate. How can there be any justice when the most beautiful celebrities allow themselves to be corrupted by such a token idol of their pitiable faith. A vampire needs no trinkets to remind him that he has immortal blood and awesome powers. To have the likes of those beautiful stars in league with me would be an irresistible treat. Then with celebrities taunting and mocking this religious nonsense, every new bit of media gossip will send the churches and their mutton-headed followers back into hopeless ambiguity where they belong. (As Dracula's maniacal grin broadens, about to erupt into hysterical laughter, the group of extras next to Dracula is addressed by one of the directors.)

Director - Okay, you posies. I want you looking sharp for this next scene. Remember, this is a party scene. I want you looking alive even though most of you are the living dead. Ha! That's a pretty good one, we might have to put it in the script. (Most of the extras groan and shake their heads.) Alright I want some of you Count Draculas here first for a quick action shot, and remember you party people, only the ones who can dance in front please. The rest just mingle or something in the back. Alright, I want you, you (pointing at extras dressed in tuxedos and capes, he points to Dracula lastly, he is wearing a very out of date plain black suit and cape... his shirt almost appears faded brown from many dried blood stains) and you. You'll do nicely (he says while eying Dracula). Wardrobe! A new shirt for the Dracula with the dead look over here! (addressing Dracula) You've really got the coffin look and the bloodshot eyes to a tee, but keep away from the coffee machine. We don't need a bloody shirt until after the staking!

Wardrobe hands Dracula a new shirt and he is herded over to a set where a scene is about to be shot. There are three coffins situated in a makeshift mausoleum. Two of the coffins already contain young nubile girls dressed sparsely in short lacy undergarments.

Dracula - (thinking to himself) 'There must be an easier way to meet a celebrity actress,' as he dons the shirt and is somewhat self-conscious entering the centrally placed casket. As final preparations for the scene are made he glances over to the revealing and ample features of his female cohorts and sighs, 'I'm glad that the needs of a vampire are still understood somewhere. This coffin is really quite comfortable, my back feels a hundred years younger.' He closes his eyes and allows himself to relax as his mind drifts into a trance-like state.

His sleep is abruptly disturbed by the muffled sound of the director barking orders through his megaphone while perched high atop a chairlift in the dark background of the set. Dracula then realizes he has forgotten to ask what his lines might be and looks over at his tantalizing coffined partners... their eyes are closed, their bodies still and white with pasty makeup but they do not appear even remotely dead to Dracula's quick eye as he follows the breathing motions of their chests and the subsequent reverberations of their thinly clad breasts. He whispers to them hoarsely...

Dracula - What do I say? I don't know my line.

Vampire girl – Shhh! Just close your eyes!

3

Just then they hear the Director say, 'Ready, set, action!' Dracula closes his eyes and feels a strange premonition of an uncertain haunting yet familiar unpleasantness. Then the voice of an actress, perhaps the star of the picture is heard. The voice is lovely and he hopes could only emanate from a very attractive throat.

Lead Actress - (softly to the others with her - two scared boyfriends) The smell is decay and death. We must be near the lair of the monster now. (They are all wearing crosses and festooned heavily with garlic. The actress also has a large purse in which she carries a wooden stake and claw hammer. They come upon the caskets and utter frightened gasps.) Look, he keeps the bodies of his victims at his side (whispering and motions to the others to keep still). We must not let ourselves fear this fiend, no matter what he might do or say. We must do what we came here to do (in one motion she brings out the stake holding it near the pointed end and positions it over Dracula's left chest). We must rid the world of this unholy evil before it is too late!

As the actress sends the hammer swiftly through its arc of motion Dracula snaps his eyes open and sees that in the next instant he will be sent to his eternal damnation. He is overcome with fear and rage at the incredible irony of the situation and feels his persistent personality complex of intimacy and betrayal kick in with a vengeance.

Just as Dracula begins a blood curdling scream in order to break the actress's eardrums and damage the sensitive inner ear affecting her sense of equilibrium, the hammer face contacts the flattened end of the stake and it appears to sink several inches into his body. It is a fake stake of course, a simple stage prop that merely retracts into itself. A considerable amount of fake blood drenches his shirt which came from a packet the actress cleverly concealed in the hand holding the stake.

Realizing with much relief what has happened or rather what had not happened, Dracula's face erupts into a toothy grin highlighting his prominent canines. He fixes his eyes on the actress with a contemptible sneer until a fresh realization dawns on him. Her arm pumping quickly, the actress raises the hammer high again. Alarms go off at a fevered pitch again in Dracula's head and he feels his sanity fall swiftly away. He has to escape. There is no time. The hammer falls again.

With renewed relief Dracula realizes he is not being exterminated as the actress's blow leaves him unscathed. Now convinced of the ploy he decides to play along and upon the third smack of the hammer he utters a raspy death gasp and grotesquely writhes in agony. Finally he is still. The actress removes her blood stained hand and stares down at him in heartfelt horror and amazement. Farther off they hear the Director yell...

Director - Cut! That's a wrap. Third times a charm. Way to hammer honey. See that, sometimes you keep going with a scene and it'll pay off. Say he's not dead is he? Just sensational. Somebody get the number of Dracula's agent if he still has a pulse, that is (laughs at his crass humor).

4

Meanwhile Dracula sits up and smiles seductively at the lead actress.

Actress - I'm glad you're okay. I really had to cover up, I mean do some real acting after that last pounding because I thought you may have been hurt.

Dracula - Seems that I had to cover up too (he says while glancing over to the young girls in negligee as they scramble out of their coffins). You see the director fellow neglected to mention that this was to be a death scene. And being a vampire, you can imagine how a stake through the heart is not on my wish list. In fact, I'd rather be hit by a truck.

Actress - Oh you don't mean that, (laughing) I'll tell you something (lowering her voice) nobody likes that director very much. He's a bitch to everyone and he upsets some of the girls too. He wouldn't dare come near me of course. If he did I'd walk out and he'd lose millions. This isn't what I need for my image anyway. (As she talks with Dracula he stares intently into her eyes and she loses her composure.) Hey, you know you really could be a vampire. I just had the strangest feeling, as if I were on my first date or something.

Dracula - Well you are certainly very lovely and very young. But it would be hard to imagine you might have been lovelier at any other time of your life, such as a first date.

Actress - Well thank you, that's a compliment I don't hear everyday. You know I've been trying to decide if you are a young looking older man or an older looking younger man. You might be anywhere from twenty-five to sixty and I wouldn't know. Isn't that strange?

Dracula - Perhaps, but that is the magic of the golden screen, is it not? How young stars mature overnight yet the older stars maintain eternal youth.

Actress - You mean silver screen. And yes I suppose that's true. With the way you talk I'd say you'd have to be older. Maybe some day I'll find out (she allows her glance to drop to Dracula's midsection as she smiles suggestively).

5

Dracula begins to fix his eyes once more into the hypnotic stare that will allow him to sink his fangs into her tender yielding neck. She does not meet his gaze however.

Actress - I've got to go and get ready for the next scene.

I'd like to see you again though. I'm having a party at my place next weekend and you're welcome to come and bring someone or whatever. (The actress leaves Dracula to tend his strained and bloodshot eyes.)

Dracula departs the set after leaving a number where he or Renfield can be reached with the Director's pesky errand boy. He takes to the air, a large dark shadow flitting overhead on an even darker night. He can risk flying high and fast on such a dark night and avoid the worry of phone or power line entanglements. He has gone too long without new blood though and can feel his wing muscles start to cramp and ache as he grows more tired from the exertion. He scans the coastline in search of a victim to fulfill his foul need.

Dracula - Hey, what's with this narrator? I'm Dracula the powerful, an immortal vampire. I don't need to take this from some second rate narrator. 'To fulfill his foul need' indeed! Excuse me for living. He gets a chance to record the world's most enduring tantalizing legend and he treats it like something you see on Police Story or Hard Copy. I've had enough!

Narrator - I beg your pardon sir, but you are a foul soulless creature spawned of the devil and tortured by the all consuming need to feed on the blood of the living.

Dracula - Watch it with that 'foul' bit already. Who says I spawned of the devil? Never mind how I was spawned. I swear if it's not Renfield's bugs, or a practical joker movie director and his errand boys, it's the damned narrator. It's always something. And right now, it's something to eat. Where are all the beach bums or girls who stare out into the ocean contemplating suicide when you need them?

Narrator - As Dracula searches desperately for his next meal he is too busy to notice the sun slowly edging its way to the brim of the horizon. He feels the first tentative rays absorbing into his raiment as an itching, distracting sensation until a thin band of yellow heat slivers its way into the center of the eastern horizon. He glances out to the ocean to notice the peculiar sparkling of the waves and the realization of his miserable state is forced upon him.

Dracula - Will you shut up for God's sake? Renfield had better be up. It's nights like these I could almost wish to be human. Then I might challenge that insufferable narrator to a fair fight, as it is I'll have to settle for snapping his insignificant neck like a twig.

6

Dracula arrives at the alcove to the door of his residence which is somewhat protected by many branches thickly shading the sun.

Dracula - (banging on the door) Renfield, open the damn door you bug brained imbecile!

Renfield - (appearing quickly at the doorway) Sorry master. Master I think you may be on fire, let me get some water. (Renfield scuttles off, while Dracula notices fine mists of smoke wafting from his cape and hair.)

Dracula - My wings would be flame broiled about now and dipped in hot sauce. Colonel Sanders would be proud. (Renfield hurries to his side and gives him liberal dosings with a bucket of water.)

Renfield - Two days in a row master. You must be more careful.

Dracula - And not only that. I haven't eaten in weeks. After conversing with that lovely actress's neck... I mean, well you know what I mean. She has excellent lines Renfield, her veins pulsed on every syllable she spoke. Ah Renfield, I could almost drain one of your vermin just thinking of it. You may have to cover your own filthy stump of a headrest before long.

Renfield - There's no need for that, master. I found a special treat for you and have tied her in the basement. But you owe me a favor now, isn't that right master? Master?

Dracula - (Dracula descends to his coffin chamber room to find a frightened young girl of no more than nine or ten. His eyes glaze over and he approaches her saying...) 'Relax little jelly donut, you won't remember a thing... Ah Renfield, Renfield you've outdone yourself!' (He slakes his hunger and repairs to his coffin allowing the dazed girl to wander back upstairs to Renfield who returns her to the nearby cemetery where he discovered her playing the previous day.)

7

That evening Dracula arises from his death-like state of repose to find Renfield in the kitchen slaving over his cooking pot once more.

Renfield - Did you enjoy my surprise Master? A nice tender morsel after your long journey?

Dracula - That was quite a surprise. I'll try to refrain from castigating you so often. How did you manage it? A box of bugs in one hand and a child in the other. I commend you, Renfield. And you mustn't concern yourself, you will probably have your wish of meeting the starring actress, Miss Brazen Gillpuppy is her name, I believe. Not the most alluring or captivating name for a star but she is a celebrity of sorts and quite a commodity with the tabloid writers of Hollywood, or so I've heard.

Renfield - Could you master? That would be wonderful, for even a little while. I saw her in Beverly Hills Corpse, it really made me squirm. By the way master, there was a message for you today from a director in charge of production asking that you please return to the set of the movie you attended yesterday. They want to try you in another scene. Master you could really become a star just like you planned. You won't forget me will you, when you're a bigger than life actor or bigger than death I mean? And maybe a small room away from the servants and guests at your new mansion in Hollywood? (Renfield applies his most pitiable, somehow beguiling expression.) That wouldn't be too much, would it master? I'm forgetting my meal worm and toad stew, please excuse me, master. (Renfield resumes cooking.)

Dracula - Yes, Renfield... (Dracula utters while apparently becoming lost in thought) We mustn't forget the purpose, the grand design so to speak... I've waited too long to have my way with these religious buffoons, the Christians, the Jews, the Hindus, the Evangelists! Can you imagine thousands of years of persecution at the hands of these simpletons, Renfield? The bitter uncanny irony of millions devoted to their religious postulations of poppycock while the vampire is spurned, no despised and tortured like an animal. I tell you I want revenge and I shall have it! (Dracula clenches his fist so hard tendons pop from their moorings at his wrist and elbow.) I hate it when that happens, it'll be an hour before I can fly.

You see, don't you Renfield, that a vampire is really not inherently evil as they believe. We really only kill as a last resort in order to avoid detection and death. Sometimes the will is strong, and a person may have some resistance at first to the effect of the bite. A responsible vampire can usually overcome this with persistence otherwise the other option of course is death, usually by overfeeding. Typically though, the careful induction of a newly formed vampire can take months in order that complete powers are developed.

Renfield - Will you be turning Miss Gillpuppy into one master?

Dracula - Yes, in all likelihood. With her tremendous popular appeal joined with the immortal vampire blood. We'll spread our legacy through the celebrity world and the lifeblood of the world's most influential country. The Dracula clan will be back in vogue before the proselytizing pulpit parrots realize that their lambs have been taken to market! I haven't felt this good since I was able to switch sacramental wine with vampirized blood in a cathedral's communion service and turned half the congregation into zombies for a day. It was a night service, of course. Even the priest loosened up and started talking about his need for the company of young boys. It was something... Well Renfield, I'm off. Wish me luck.

Renfield - Good luck Master, I'll leave the door open. Be careful, studio lights can be very bright. (Dracula has already taken his leave, rapidly knifing his way through the night's sky with great vigor.)

8

Dracula arrives on the set once more feeling hale and hearty, appearing much younger than the ancient visage of a vampire he is. He's greeted warmly by a group of extras who envied his startling performance the night before. The director spies him and calls him over.

Director - Good, you've come! Tonight we want to try something a little experimental Count. You don't mind if I call you Count Dracula? Of course you don't, you can't put enough importance on living the role, or dying in this case. Anyway you already know that better than the rest of these vampires, don't you? (Dracula nods tolerantly) Of course, you do. Well, we'd like to shoot a scene that occurs earlier in the picture naturally since you've already been staked. Sounds kind of funny to say that doesn't it? Might have to put a line like that in the script. God, I love the way I talk. Anyway, that's the magic of the movies, isn't it? (Dracula nods while shifting his eyes inquisitively) Yes, to make a movie all you have to do is patch and paste, paste and patch. The order of the scenes isn't important until the shootings over. So here's what we got ...

9

The shooting proceeds smoothly with Dracula portraying the prominent vampire role, even to the point of reshooting earlier scenes to heighten the effect of Dracula"s featured role. He romances Buffy, played by Brazen Gillpuppy, so arduously that medics must be called to revive her. She complains that her heart feels like it's fluttering and she's given a mild tranquilizer by the company's doctor. All the while crude stage hands leer at each other with understanding smiles.

1st Extra - (remarking to a fellow actor) Wait'll we see the tabloid report about this. Brazen Gillpuppy swept helplessly off her feet by real life Dracula on the set of her new movie. Must be resuscitated from love swoon during the filming of scenes with her new leading man, a centuries old vampire. Ha!

2nd Extra - Hey, don't be so hard on him. He can't help it if he's got it.

1st Extra - Rumor has it that half the production staff has what it takes to satisfy Miss Gillpuppy. I wonder what would make her flip out over a new actor nobody's ever heard of?

2nd Extra - Maybe she just wants him to notice her.

1st Extra - No, no... I think it's something more basic, more physical maybe even primal. Did you see his eyes? You know how contacts are only supposed to color the iris. Well even his pupils look red, if he has them at all.

2nd Extra - You're just seeing things. He might have some kind of special contacts like the ones Michael Jackson wore in Thriller!

1st Extra - No, really... and there was no reflection when he walked by the mirrors. You're not supposed to see the special effects while they're shooting! They add that in later.

2nd Extra - I don't know, he probably had a triple garlic pizza before the shoot and his breath just knocked her cold!

1st Extra - Yea you're probably right. That must be it. (both laugh)

10

Just then Dracula strides offstage to the area where most of the supporting actors and extras have collected to discuss their scenes and munch on pastries leftover from the producers and directors.

Dracula - (announcing suavely) I'd like you all to know that Miss Gillpuppy is fine... merely a case of butterfly stomach from her meatless diet, no doubt (scattered laughter) and she will be back on her feet tomorrow unless of course the script calls for a bed scene. (more laughter) She asked me to tell you that you are all invited to a party at her estate this weekend. (subdued cheers) There will be entertainment - the torturing of innocents (cheers), and food - the killing and roasting of dumb animals (cheers), libation - as many bloody Mary's as you can drink (cheers), and last but not least - the rites of passage into eternal life as a vampire administered by Brazen and myself (loud cheers).

11

The scene now shifts back to Dracula's residence where it has been several weeks since what he refers to as 'his movie' has completed filming. Brazen's party with Dracula's malevolent flair for decadence was a huge success and lasted three days. We find him mulling over the situation with Renfield in his attempt to forecast an imminent horrific decay of status quo humanity and the destruction of society's basic religious and social standards of decency and morals.

Dracula - Huge success? I think not. And who does this narrator think he is pretending to know the mind of Dracula? I swear if I don't have his liver on a plate before long, I'll probably develop a blood pressure.

Renfield - Yes master, do you think Miss Gillpuppy will visit today?

Dracula - Renfield, you've been asking that same question every night for the last three weeks. I told you these things take time. She seemed very susceptible to the bite at first but these Hollywood people are a strange breed. She appears to lack the ideals of trust and dependency which would allow for intimacy, even rudimentary intimacy needed to fully experience the effect of the bite. The normal mating-bonding values aren't there. She even confided to me that she actually prefers the affection of her pets to her friends. She might have instinctively sensed that I too am not human. Regardless, it will be a very difficult conversion indeed.

The Reemergence of Vlad!

Renfield - I am sorry to hear that master. Maybe if you were to tell her about my nest of baby moles. I am trying to train them to see by only feeding them during the day. They are very cute I would hate to have to eat them, though I know they would be delicious with some herbs and butter.

Dracula - That's an idea, you raving sot but it wouldn't do to have her visit and become disillusioned about life as a vampire before the transformation.

Renfield - Yes master, but if we're to be moving soon didn't you say that it might not hurt to take some risks? I'm sure it would be exciting.

Dracula - You're right Renfield, I'm behaving like a scared relic, an anachronism out of time with this world. It's time this world had a more liberal dose of Count Dracula and the manifestations of my destiny. Besides, even though I initiated most of the actors and movie production people at the party there is little chance they could become vampires. These movie people are just too hard to locate, they have their agents and publicity managers. They have people that handle the people that handle them. After this, they're all going in different directions, starting new projects. No, I'd better shoot for the top. Once this Gillpuppy star is immortal, they'll be no stopping us. Eh, Renfield? And you can help!

Renfield - No, master, I mean yes master. What should I do?

Dracula - Maybe I am starting to slip. In the old days, three bites tops and they'd be mine forever. Now it's rationalize this, philosophize that, really nothing more than finding excuses. Renfield, I'm going to have to entice her here, give her the maximum bite and hope she'll live. If she does she'll likely be too weak to leave but you can see to it that she doesn't. If you can guard her long enough, she won't be able to withstand successive extraction-infusions of the substance of her soul. And she'll be ours, body and soul for all eternity to do with what we please.

Renfield - Master, please I can't stand it! It's so exciting master, I'm not worthy of you. (Renfield grunts and snorts with pleasure.)

Dracula - Control, Renfield, we must work before we can reap the rewards. First, I think I should perform the old exercises a while so that my venomous kiss might have its peak potency. (Dracula picks up a freshly cut two by four from a pile on one side of the room, clamps it tightly in the center with his formidable teeth and jaws, and neatly snaps off both ends with a firm grip from his hands. He repeats this maneuver several times then recruits Renfield's aid for more jaw isometric routines. Renfield braces himself then pushes both palms against one side of Dracula's face, while Dracula using only his jaw muscles easily withstands the full force of Renfield's body. Renfield nearly collapses afterward from the exertion.)

Renfield - Please don't be angry with me master. I am only an animal compared to you and not a very good one. You are in awfully good condition with teeth like a tiger's.

Dracula - I feel good at that. I could probably bring down an elephant if I had to. But it's a very special prey I seek and must be ready. She could very well test my limits. I'll ask her to come tonight and you must remember to play your part my friend.

Renfield - Oh yes, yes I will master.

Dracula - If I leave a sufficient residue of my blood in her veins she will sleep most of the day. But if she wakes you must be waiting for her. You may use any means at your disposal but do not make a sexual attack on her nor injure her where she loses any blood. Do you understand Renfield?

Renfield - Yes, yes, but a sexual attack, master?

Dracula - You know, what your filthy bugs and rats do to make more rats, baby rats. Surely you've seen the movies often enough to know... I'm surprised at you Renfield.

Renfield - Yes, a sexual attack! (almost slobbering)

Dracula - No! No sexual attack! You must not, she will be too weak and then the transformation could kill her.

Renfield - I understand, master.

Dracula - I hope you do. Now off with you until she sleeps.

(Renfield scuttles off to an obscure part of the house to tend his bugs while Dracula goes out to phone Mistress Gillpuppy. Ringing her estate...) Hello is this Miss Gillpuppy's estate?

Secretary - Yes.

Dracula - Is Miss Gillpuppy at home? This is Count Dracula her co-star in the new movie...

Secretary - Oh, Mr. Dracula, hold on a minute.

Dracula - That's Count Dracula... (the secretary has already put Dracula on hold) How rude... If they're going to permit servants to use these devices they should be trained in the proper manner.

Brazen Gillpuppy - This is Miss Gillpuppy. Is that you Count?

Dracula - Yes, I would like you to come visit me at my home tonight,

Brazen - You would? I thought you decided that a courtship as you call it was in order before I see your home.

Dracula - Yes well there were things I had to take care of here but they've been attended to. It is a matter of utmost urgency. I'd like to see you right away.

Brazen - (acting coyly) I don't know Count, if it's about the movie, you know my agent always handles everything.

Dracula - This doesn't concern the movie. It's rather a personal matter.

Brazen - Don't tell me... You have tremendous women problems? The neighborhood girls have heard you've starred in a movie and they've been flocking to your door like bats to a cave. I don't mean to say you're like a cave. You're really more like a large craggy mountain top with forests and lots of woodland animals scurrying about.

Dracula - This is a more serious matter.

Brazen - Serious as some honey is to a nest of bees. Just show those girls some tooth and let them know you can sting back! No really Count, if you'd like to talk or something more serious like you say I'd be happy to come (says with a purr in her voice).

Dracula - (muttering to himself setting down the phone) Well I handled that magnificently, I feel as I'm the one about to be filleted and hung out to dry.

12

The evening passes and it starts to get late. Then there is a knock on the door. The large front door with wolf's head engraving creaks open and Brazen stands in the entranceway. She wears a black silky minidress, and a sheer black lace undergarment easily apparent from the loose fit at the shoulders. A large plain silver cross rests comfortably at the crook of her breasts.

Brazen - (calling) Count, Count? You know this is a pretty bad area, I wouldn't be surprised if you were worried about the neighbors. You're still playing the vampire bit aren't you? Somehow I'm not surprised. Oh there you are.

Dracula - (appears before her from within the gloom of the darkened inner rooms of the house) Good evening.

Brazen - You know everyone kind of realized that you had a real feeling for your role, that you may have been living it too closely. This place might give Norman Bates the creeps. And remember at the party when you wouldn't take off your teeth or makeup? And those vampire initiation rites, some of the fellows thought it was too much. I don't know if you realized it but those dental daggers of yours actually gave some of the girls nasty cuts.

Dracula - Yes, I am sorry about that... (he sweeps his cape and arm around her shoulders dwarfing her diminutive figure and leads her to a central room of the house) The role does seem to be second nature to me... I've lived it a very long time.

Brazen - Alright Mr. Vampire, Mr. Icewater veins and pasty chalk makeup, Mr. I'm a thousand years old and going on two thousand, just what is this about? (Dracula seats her beside him on the oddly shaped oblong couch)

Dracula - Why I think you have already guessed. Eternity can be a very long time and it wouldn't do for someone of your charm and consummate beauty not to experience it with me. (As he speaks the last few words he grabs her arms above the elbows paralyzing them at her sides. He stares deeply into her eyes and from the force of his stare and his grip she arches obscenely toward him and exposes her soft supple neck, her jugular vein quickly filled with blood. He hesitates a moment to revel at his conquest then falls precipitously upon her deftly clamping his jaw on her neck and neatly piercing her jugular with his protruding newly sharpened canines. She can't move for fear of further harming her neck and utters pitiable moaning sounds as a sign of weak acquiescence. Just as Dracula begins to drink he starts to notice a burning sensation at the center of his chest and recalls that Brazen had been wearing a large silver cross on her neck chain. The pain intensifies and he must release his quarry.)

Dracula - This won't do at all! (He croaks while pawing fiercely at the chain and flinging the cross away.)

Brazen - (catching her breath) I'm really not into this Count or whoever you are. Listen, why don't we discuss it when we're both feeling better? (She silently slips her hand into her purse and presses a signal button that accesses her private security system. Dracula tosses her purse aside and considers her as she backs away with her torn dress draped on one shoulder.)

The Reemergence of Vlad!

Dracula - (with glazed reddened eyes)   Your heritage transcends acceptance or denial. It is given, nothing more. (He lunges and ensnares her once more in his vice-like grasp. She struggles and kicks slipping partly off the couch which is actually a padded coffin top but only succeeds in exposing her shapely legs and hips to the watchful eyes of Renfield cautiously waiting in the next room.

Dracula once more applies his bite to her fresh wounds and she is quickly subdued. He drinks freely and Miss Gillpuppy is soon rendered unconscious from the transfusion effect, the intermingling of blood that has occurred between Dracula and herself.   Her drained blood supply resulting in hypovolemia and an oxygen-starved brain serve to further her trip to oblivion.

Dracula returns to his coffin chamber leaving the helpless star at the mercy of Renfield's demented fantasies.

Renfield - (whispering close to her ear) Don't worry Miss Puppy I will take very good care of you, but you must behave. Master doesn't want to hurt you, either. Not like the others. You are very special. You'll see later when you are a vampire. Master will be very pleased. (He starts to drool as he appraises her attractive limp body. He adjusts her position and prepares to tie her securely then momentarily loses control and begins to excitedly lick her knee then checks himself and returns to his task.)

13

The abducted star remains asleep throughout the day and Renfield keeps frequent tabs on her while making another breakthrough in insect culinary science. At the first signs of dusk she begins to stir and opens her eyes. She remembers Dracula's maniac behavior and the wounds on her neck and realizes that another encounter of the vampire-kind could be her last. Her skin already appears deathly white and she is still light-headed. She notices the aroma from Renfield's cooking and wonders if it might be snails, mussels or some other equally disgusting fare. Suddenly the normally worrisome sound of a police siren peals through the quiet early evening air of Dracula's remote district and rapidly approaches until it can be heard clearly fixating outside Dracula's residence.

14

Moments later the sound of rapping resounds loudly throughout the house.

Lieutenant Officer - Alright in there, open the door. We know you have actress Brazen Gillpuppy against her will. (One of the other officers mutters 'we hope!' The lieutenant motions for him to shut up.) And there are men stationed around the house. You have one more minute.

Renfield - (Renfield answers the door, hunching over obsequiously.) Hello officers, I hope there hasn't been any trouble. I don't think there has been any here. Maybe you have the wrong address? Did you double check the number?

Lieutenant - No we didn't. Listen Bub, we did some checking before we came out here. You don't have a phone or an address number.

Renfield - Is that against the law officer?

Lieutenant - No the point is actress Gillpuppy, who you've got... Listen I don't have to explain, just step back please.

Renfield - My master doesn't permit... (Renfield is shunted to one side as several large officers enter.)

Miss Gillpuppy - Over here, officers. (The officers try to find their way through the dark and thickly shadowed rooms with flashlights and discover the actress tethered to the couch.)

Captain - Are you alright Miss Gillpuppy?

Brazen - Yes but please untie me, I'm glad my homing signal still works. I don't think I could have lasted another day.

Captain - I take it you'd like to press charges on this weirdo. (The captain grabs Renfield who has followed them and shakes him violently.)

Brazen - No not him, I'm not even sure who that is. This is the first I've seen him. He may be the housekeeper, I suppose.

Lieutenant - He certainly doesn't keep house very well. How about turning the lights on Bub?

Renfield - I'm sorry, my master doesn't permit it. He prefers...

Dracula - (startles the officers by his silent entrance) That will be fine, Renfield. (then to the captain) Please, try not to hurt him, it is his physical or rather medical condition which renders him the pitiable creature you see.

Brazen - That's him, officers. He invited me here on a pretense. He was the leading man in my latest movie but he's a sicko. Look at these! (Two of the officers shine their lights on her breasts, only the Lieutenant notices the small wounds on her neck.)

Lieutenant - (coughing) Excuse me Miss Brazen, it does appear you may have had a rough night.

Dracula - (interrupting) Yes Brazen and I have been quite intimate on the movie set and when she accepted my invitation to visit, as I'm sure you noticed her car parked nearby, well I guess I may have let my emotions get the best of me.

Lieutenant - Well yes, I certainly see how that may have occurred but if Miss Gillpuppy (cough) wants to press charges I'm afraid we'll have to take a trip down to the station. Will that be the case Miss Brazen?

Brazen - Of course, you don't seem to realize that I almost died, he probably drained half my blood!   (All the officers start coughing.) I don't know what he did with it, probably drank it, the sicko. (She glowers in Dracula's direction.)

Lieutenant - Right then, (addressing Dracula) I guess we don't need your servant fellow since Miss Brazen doesn't seem to have any complaints about him.

The Reemergence of Vlad!

The next day's headlines read:

Horror Movie's Mistress Gillpuppy Ravaged by Leading Man Vampire Style: Seeks Charges and Publicity!!

15

The following evening at Dracula's residence...

Dracula - And you did get a chance to meet Miss Gillpuppy didn't you?

Renfield - Yes master, she was ever so nice. I wanted to touch her and lick her and bite...

Dracula - That'll be enough, it was fortunate her agent convinced her to withdraw the charges against me. I'm glad I didn't have to upset those police fellows had I been obliged to escape.

Renfield - Yes, another close one, master.

Dracula - How would you like to move to Hollywood, Renfield? We'll have to be careful, but now that I'm on the verge of movie stardom and a star with a knack for publicity I might add, I can continue my quest to restore my name to its rightful glory. It may be a little lonely at first, having the distinction as the only celebrity vampire, and servant of course, but at least we'll have our fans, eh Renfield?

Renfield - How exciting! Would I have fans too master? Maybe some of the smaller ones?

Richard Reich

Dracula - I don't know, we'll see...

PART II

DRACULA ... REVISITED

Dracula sits musing on Christmas eve at his new address in Hollywood...

Dracula - Life is one long bitter draught of existence, isn't it Renfield? (Renfield is by his side sitting on a faded oriental rug that came with the house, and is attentively monitoring a beetle's progress as it traverses the fibers.)

Renfield - I'm sorry to hear that, master. (staring at the insect...) But at least you are a vampire and probably one of the first, a leader or maybe even a sort of king from the legends of history. I still remember some things my father told me of the Renfield family tree as well as your own plentiful stories, master. I don't think anyone could doubt them.

Dracula - Of course they are true, true enough... *my* stories that is. I wouldn't care to conjecture about the interpretations the Renfield family has passed down. (He gazes with undisguised condescending pity toward his servant.) But Dracula is a name, not unlike other names and not a reward in itself... Just as unending life is more a curse at times than anything else. Especially at this time of year, it's just too depressing.

Renfield - You should always be glad of your power, master! Knowing that you can rip into the throats of your rivals at will must be comforting though probably does carry a certain kind of responsibility... You don't want to be relentlessly hunted down as a cold-hearted monster! Anyway you can be glad that we've arrived safely... I don't think you were much disturbed in the train's baggage compartment. I put the conductors at ease telling them that the winter weather would be ideal for my special cargo, a deceased corpse! They were most ready to oblige me.

Dracula - That's good, Renfield. I was wondering during my brief late night walks on the trip whether any conductors had happened to spy the contents of the coffin. It's too bad none had really... it would have given me good reason to take some nourishing blood.

Renfield - Not to worry master. There is an entire city to dine on. Los Angeles is one of the largest in the world! And here in the hills of Hollywood there may be all manner of creature... Do you think there may be vampires as well? I for one do not intend to do much venturing at night! (He pricks up his ears as if listening for unseen enemies.)

Dracula - There may well be vampires in this area, a center of culture and entertainment, movie stars and television. The fastest of lifestyles should be found here and what could be more appealing to a vampire than such excitement after the boredom of existence begins to take its toll?

Renfield - Yes master, and your new house seems to be very exciting as well. It looks much better than its picture in the brochure.

Dracula - An estate sale of course. I feel much better knowing the previous owner has recently died. (He winces while watching Renfield consume a bug he'd been tending for obscenely long moments.) That and the fact that probate court prices offer good bargains sometimes. A fact lost on most decent and god-fearing home buyers.

Renfield - You are quite wise, master. (smiling)

Dracula - Thank you, it is a helpful habit. (He pulls his eyes from Renfield as the servant lets loose another crawling quarry on the large carpet.) I also took the precaution of traveling by rail rather than air due to the remarkable frequency that cargo is lost or sent on erroneous flights, to be quarantined and examined. It would be very upsetting to be awakened during a midday rush at some crowded customs counter!

Renfield - I would have my work cut out then, but they would have to torture me I promise!

Dracula - Don't worry, there will be plenty of other times for that but for now we are safe. So tonight I will let you take stock of the house, maybe put a few things in order... You probably have things to take care of in the kitchen anyway. For myself though I plan to dine out this evening... (Renfield's face shows some anxiety as he pries it away from the small creature's frenzy of activity.) But no need for the exercises. (Renfield looks relieved.)

Renfield - Good hunting master. I'll prepare your resting chamber for you and please remember to return early as these are new surroundings and will be unfamiliar for a while. (Dracula has already departed while Renfield returns attentions to his prize and continues to talk, used to his master's hasty habit.) And especially if you travel too far. Well I suppose you'll have ways of finding direction. You always do even without lights and signs, but remember all those close calls! (Suddenly bored he snatches up the bug and swallows quickly, rises then checks on the door after his master's exit.) I wish he would let me put up at least one light... (Renfield mutters as he wanders through the ghostly spacious moonlit rooms and the darker rambling interior halls of wainscoted wood paneling and water-stained wall paper in search of undisturbed webbings and sudden small scurryings within the old house set amidst the rolling hills of suburban Hollywood. The geography is aptly named, sporting impressively high hills and lying just south of Hollywood itself, and of course home to more than a handful of stellar celebrities and movie stars.

1

Dracula soars through the night sky, high over Hollywood Hills, flitting against the darkened landscape... as an erratic shadow of some large misshapen bat might appear. He does not fear detection.

He knows that Hollywood's hi-tech wizardry and special effects movie sets, however awe-inspiring, are merely glitter without substance. Most of the really advanced atmospheric monitoring devices remain the province of NASA based programs in Florida and Texas. And those agencies have carefully distanced themselves and their professional secrets from Hollywood. Constant worries about loss of respect and integrity plague the men of science should the madcap movie moguls succeed in duplicating actual aerospace technology. But even if someone could detect him it's doubtful a flying form resembling an oversized bat might raise undue concern, appearing almost a shadow flitting by across the landscape in the night.

As his limbs begin to tire he notices a large wooded estate, if palm trees can be considered authentic trees, and makes a swooping descent. He reforms near a clearing some fifty yards from the mansion but in the direct presence of a young and obviously beautiful girl who is reclined on a lounge chair wearing a swimsuit over which she has just the sweat pants portion of a designer sweat suit.

Dracula - (uttering quickly) Good evening.

Girl - (glancing up with a surprised start) Oh hi. (laughs) I almost just jerked my head off. I guess I've had enough champagne tonight, I didn't hear you at all. (She eyes him quizzically.) Are you one of father's guests? I thought everyone had left.

Dracula - Why yes, my name is Dracula, Count Dracula. I have a habit of retiring later than most. I was just admiring the view. You have a wonderful fog cloud over here... (He takes a couple of steps to where dense fog is thickly rising from a heated ground level pool. He realizes his mistake too late and plunges abruptly into the motionless water. The girl jumps up to help him out.) Thank you. (Releasing a hold on her tender arm, his eyes glow red for a moment then subside.) An interesting effect, I should have remembered from the movies... thoughtless.

Girl - Here, take my towel. Wow, have you really been in movies? Probably comedies right? (She laughs.) No, really I know you're talking about vampires... and Count Dracula. I've heard about him, though there are so many movies you know, you hardly have a chance to see them all even if you want to.

Dracula - (dries himself briefly)   Yes, that's unfortunate but at least now there should be plenty of actual vampires and some with real experience for this new picture. You're very perceptive for your age. I'm sure you'd make a good subject for the screen yourself...)

Girl - That's what Daddy says sometimes. 'Maybe someday,' he'll say. And oh excuse me, my name is Darla. Daddy calls me Darling but it's really Darla, Darla Spielberg. (Dracula locks his gaze on her own.) That'd be nice wouldn't it, the screen. (She says somewhat dazed.) Father says I should... Anyway I'm sorry you fell in. I was just swimming myself, the water's so nice and warm... (Dracula stares.) You know a few laps to get the blood going. (She says while trying to look away, then closing her eyes...) And I like the lights out so I can see the moon... (She seems transfixed looking to the moon, her neck exposed... Dracula apprises her supple young body, the gentle rise and fall of her intercostal and diaphragmatic muscles as she breathes.)

Dracula - (whispering) You're right, the sky is a lovely dark blue tonight, and this perfect night reflects the hidden sun almost as brightly as the moon herself. You certainly won't mind if I come closer. Your neck... I must...

Darla - I guess not... (Dracula is on her in an instant, gently attacking the cervical area, enveloping her with his cape. She appears almost completely enshrouded in darkness except for her head which moves like a small porcelain mask floating freely. Feeling her heart beating, he finishes and sets her back on the chair reminding her she will not remember the interlude but only that there is a wonderful new actor, of course, named Dracula, whom everyone will love. (She tries to rouse, weakly repeating his command) Dradilva... everyone will lub, must lud him, musb made them lud him! (She passes out.)

Dracula - (thinking) Very sweet and so easily snared... she has felt the hypnotic presence before. Maybe her father has influenced her in the ways of a vampire, maybe she drinks from others herself? No, not from the taste... (He checks the bottle she had been drinking to be sure it isn't blood.) I will have to remember this name... Spielberg.

2

Within minutes Dracula is rapidly whisking along the tops of trees and tall spear shaped shrubs scouring the terrain for signs of life. He passes over Mulholland Drive several times as it twists and turns along the summits of adjoining hills which could more accurately be termed small mountains. The canyon roads which lead up to the circuitous summit drive also provide an assessment of the real estate arranged below. Dracula's attention however is quickly diverted to the lights and sounds of Hollywood itself which lies to the south and at the foothills of the wooded mountainous region containing isolated private estates and high rent domiciles.

Hollywood in contrast is a profusion of commercial lights and cars jamming the lanes of its main boulevards, namely Hollywood and Sunset. He grins inwardly at the sights of Sunset Boulevard below, thinking that this indeed appears to be a city after his own heart... a heart not in the emotional human sense but as an immortal organ, again in the pink, flushed with the blood of a young girl. Large membranous wings flap effortlessly over the panorama of the entertainment district which makes up most of what people refer to as Hollywood. He considers landing for a moment amidst the odd collection of characters waiting at the doors to loud music playing bar houses, or comedy halls. He might not even need bother about his great black wings as they could go unnoticed against the background of unusual human costumes proliferating the sidewalks. He decides that this sort of fun can wait however and instead checks further looking for less populated areas where future meals might be encountered. Fortunately only blocks south of the main boulevards the avenues are almost completely darkened and marked profusely with potholes and overripe garbage. And better still there are rundown tenement buildings, frequent taverns and smaller playhouses whose only advertisements are paper placards pasted over the graffiti filled walls. 'A haven to be sure,' Dracula muses. 'And a wonder I haven't discovered this sooner!'

3

Pleased with what he has seen of Hollywood, Dracula returns home and soon finds himself in the main room of his large weathered estate. Renfield rushes to his side.

Renfield - I heard the noise and hurried to the door but you had already come in. There is no lock that can hold you is there master? You are also back early... I hope you were able to find sustenanch, sustemants (stammering)... blood!

Dracula - Yes I was, thanks for your concern Renfield. (He pats Renfield's head, sweeping by him and settling into a large armchair from which arise billowing clouds of dust.) I hope you will see about more adequate locks or whatever is necessary... I've become used to a heavier door with iron bolts and now these simple buttons and knobs. The sound was just my surprise at being able to open the door and then rapping my wings on the top of the doorway before remembering to reassimilate them. You have to take into account a touch of senility that comes with perpetual existence. The oldest mortals attaining only a fraction of my age are often as dumb as a bean you know. Still I choose to think my occasional lapses are due more to eccentricities and distractions than to outright mental deficit...

Renfield - Yes master, I will see to the locks. Maybe I can have someone send our old door? Yes and I have already found some keys...

Dracula - (continuing with his thoughts) It does worry me at times... this question of senility. (Renfield's attention is diverted to the action of a spider on its web in a ceiling corner. He leaps.) There was a time that with the exception of having any sort of satisfaction from eating food, I would still feel some of the tantalizing effect from powerful addicting drugs and many of the finely made fermentations and distillations of the day. Then after a while, just centuries, I hardly even noticed their presence in a victim's blood... just as with that minx tonight. Her veins probably ran with more champagne than water. I suppose it just means that I am now so attuned to these effects that they no longer hold much interest for me and are therefore simply ignored.

Renfield - Yes but at least you never get tired from the thrill of tasting the life as it is wriggling in your hand. (Renfield ravenously gulps down the captured spider he's been holding.)

Dracula - (turning abruptly away after glancing at Renfield) I trust you have seen to the luggage, Renfield?

Renfield - We had no luggage except for the contents of your crate. Remember master? You thought people might take too much notice if I were to bring clothes filled with lice and ticks, or my cooking tools that might hint at the smell of meal worm casserole? (Dracula grimaces slightly.)

Dracula - I'm sure that was the right decision. You were in need of some new things anyway. I suggest you shop for them at the earliest opportunity.

Renfield - Thank you master. I've already found wonderful things in the attic. Trunks containing all sorts of clothing with wigs and costumes and shoes as well. There may even be black capes and suits trimmed in the style you prefer. And best of all there were things left in the kitchen and a very good supply of large roaches.

Dracula - That will be enough for this evening Renfield. I'm glad you've gotten everything to your liking. If you will just show me the coffin. (Renfield follows Dracula into the hallway.) We can continue our talk tomorrow night... (As Dracula utters his 'goodnights' Renfield directs him to a darkened doorway through which he enters quickly only to discover a steep set of stairs which he has badly misjudged, winding up on the cellar floor in a rumpled heap.)

Renfield - (calling after him) And please be careful master, the stairs are quite steep. And don't worry I will have a sturdy door made for the cellar at once! Are you there, master?

The Reemergence of Vlad!

Dracula - If not Renfield with his habits, then the simple stairs and doors. Maybe I really am aging... (He says, speaking to himself. As he finds the coffin and settles to his rest he hears Renfield from above...)

Renfield - Is it too dark, master? Maybe just a couple lamps, it's only due to the bills you don't like electricity and those postal people that meddle. But I have lamps that use oil! I found them upstairs... (He says loudly and ambles away, while Dracula grits his teeth and tries to repose within his casket.)

Dracula - (whispering) And they used to call me Dracula the Tyrant, the awesome power of ancient evil... the undying Fiend! Now it will be Dracula, the crippled actor, and his miscreant unmanageable housekeeper.

4

The next evening Dracula continues his morose self-effacing and introspective diatribe... He is seated in a small room adjacent Renfield's kitchen.

Dracula - You see how it will be, don't you Renfield? People will say, 'there is Dracula, the one who rules the night but is subdued by doorways... mastered by his own servants!'

Renfield - I'm sorry, master. Please don't kill me, I promise I will try harder. It was very difficult to bring your coffin downstairs without spilling the soil. But I did it for you, master. I also did something else today...

Dracula - Don't tell me, you fell from a window so you might share my pain or better, from the roof?

Renfield - That is a funny joke (smothering a chuckle) but no, I was only thinking that with this extra large house and all the empty rooms, maybe you might afford another servant. Now that you're an actor there will be many new tasks and errands in the city and I have much work here in the house.

Dracula - So what are you trying to say, that you've found a new friend, on this the first day in Hollywood? How gregarious of you Renfield! And a welcome change from your usual self-absorbing habits, I should say.

Renfield - Not exactly. I was just minding my own business, really doing something for you, master, but there were several visitors... I was in the yard uncovering a groundhog burrow. I thought it might interest you for breakfast.

Dracula - Thanks but no, Renfield. I will probably not dine on animals anytime soon. You are welcome to dispose of the creatures in the yard as you see fit, please go on.

Renfield - It would be no trouble to squeeze some juice into a glass. I've got him in the large white box, what is called the ice box or refrigerator. He's there now. It was quite a struggle!

Dracula - I don't doubt it, being a few sizes larger than your usual prey. (looking concerned) Doesn't that unit require electricity though? You'd just have to deliver payments every month unless they would agree to some kind of advance schedule. Is that who you met today, one of those bothersome postmen?

Renfield - No, just two neighbors at first and they brought some unusual things for us to eat, a large cake and a bag of grounded beans for coffee!

The Reemergence of Vlad!

Dracula - Apparently useless items, but you may keep them if you like. It worries me though Renfield. I should have chosen a more remote location, even these secluded wooded hills are infested with people. What did you do with these neighbors then?

Renfield - Nothing master, but don't worry because I didn't say anything about you. They had already seen you themselves, sometime last night, they said. Anyway today they were very curious. I didn't want to let them in but they had presents and I thought they might stop asking their questions if I let them in. Then I was going to lock them in one of the rooms because they kept asking about you but I couldn't fit the right keys... so they left on their own.

Dracula - I suppose if you had kept them out it might only make things worse with the way they would gossip. It's much the same everywhere in that regard, even the old country. I'll tell you more stories someday, you'll be amazed. My neighbors in Transylvania were actually of the firm belief that I stood eight feet tall, had enormous webbed wings stretching twenty feet and could kill a man with the merest kiss to the neck! For the most part they were right, their beliefs were to me an elixir but in time I grew to detest them because they soon used these fanciful accounts to suit their purposes, blaming me for their own trivial misdeeds and failings. And to successive generations I became more a hopeless though fearsome vagrant than the vampire of legend.

Renfield - It will be different here in Hollywood, won't it?

Dracula - I don't see how it couldn't. The magic of Hollywood combined with mine should be enough to stop the loosed tongues wagging... the insipid flapping of mouths. Soon Renfield, the quivering eyes of those who would mock me will freeze with fear! Their wretched minds will seize the truth...

Renfield - And cease their lying, right master? But wasn't it 'vacant minds?'

Dracula - Vacant minds... lying... I guess I've repeated that speech a little too often haven't I? I've been practicing that rant hundreds of years, and not realizing... except for the part about Hollywood of course. The first time... mm I gave vent to my hatred outside of war and the stakings, such glorious stakings. Anyway it was around the time I first left the castle of my ancestors and also your ancestors as well Renfield. I was very frustrated then with all the prejudice and the religious fervor against me, and unfortunately haven't had much reason to be otherwise since. Though I guess I did do well for a while in some of the less restrictive locales such as Spain and France... Hawaii was nice. Did I tell you I was well liked in Hawaii, Renfield? But why is it the most alluring places have the impossible languages? (Dracula appears to have hypnotized himself with reminiscences. Renfield is slightly irritated.)

Renfield - That's nice master, but I haven't finished about the visitors...

Dracula - You don't think they'll be causing any trouble?

Renfield - Probably not the ones who left... the ones I told you about, but there was another later, a young girl... She got upset when she saw me catch the groundhog. I didn't know she was there... in the next yard and the sound of my snorting quarry was loud and irritating even to me, I admit. She wanted it put back so I had to tell her that we often keep animals safely in the house. I just couldn't let it go after such a long fight. So then I invited her in, and when she was in the house I told her to wait in the main room but she knew I meant to put my catch in the refrigerator unit... (He pauses.) I had to attack her master. And now we have both a groundhog and a neighbor at once! A full course meal, master?

Dracula - Renfield, really you amaze me! I can't imagine that I'll be in the mood for a burrowing rodent anytime soon. I had a bit of luck and dined last evening, and I'm certain this area will hold as much promise as I've hoped. I'd like to see our new neighbor though. If you haven't hurt her too badly, I'll see what I can do about convincing her to be your friend.

Renfield - Yes, I'd like that very much! But I haven't had many friends before and she hasn't liked me much up until now...

Dracula - Don't worry, I'll see to it... but it will help if you try to find something in common with her. Where is she? (Renfield leads Dracula to the main room where Renfield has pinned the dazed girl under a sofa on which are stacked several large cushioned chairs.) Perhaps if you stop your practice of hoarding animals in the house you may find time for a friend to share this mutual fascination or whatever it is you feel toward these bothersome creatures. (With Renfield's pointing Dracula locates where the girl is confined within the furniture and notices that she is indeed young and attractive. She hears their approach and begins to struggle frantically against the massive old-style furniture Renfield has chosen to pile about her in sort of a makeshift tomb.)

Girl - Please don't kill me. I'll do anything you want, anything! I know how expensive things are trying to keep up a house... (She glances around at the dust-laden room) and just getting a decent meal these days. I don't care if you eat that groundhog, honest! But just let me go, I swear I won't tell... (She looks at Renfield who is grinning a bit too widely and her terror mounts.) I once saw someone catch a goose down at the Griffith's park by the pond but I never told on him, honest I didn't! Please, I know a lot of girls only care about money you know, going out on expensive dates at the clubs... I'm not like that.

Dracula - And after all, this is Hollywood, the nightlife cannot be ignored.

Girl - (sweating nervously) True, so true. And you can tell right, that I'm not that type of girl, can't you? I don't mean I don't like to go out now and then, who doesn't right? But I don't make a guy spend his paycheck you understand. So don't you think we'd have a better time if we went out somewhere first? It could be anywhere really. Then maybe come back to the house later... Besides, it's way too early yet, I mean for this sort of thing, isn't it?

Renfield - She is very nice, ever so, isn't she? (He apprises her earnestly.)

Dracula - Yes Renfield. (then addressing the girl) Your idea is entertaining, my dear, but I'm afraid we don't have need of things like the paychecks you mentioned.

Girl - Oh (softly) I was afraid of that... but couldn't we do something less brutal, it doesn't matter much what, even down by the beach. A nice walk by the waves, at night you can hardly notice any pollution. (Dracula remains frozen, considering her situation and apparently lost in thought. She pauses and continues meekly...) We're not going out then are we?

Dracula - (In a swift motion Dracula sends the ornate bulky furniture thudding across the room. The girl jumps up and he imprisons her tightly in his grasp. His hands deftly work the pressure points at the elbows sending her delicate nerves into a state of paralytic excitement and the sensation of weight and movement seem to drain from her body. Her chest and neck reflexively respond arching and yielding themselves up to his waiting mouth. As his great teeth sink into the buttery flesh of her neck she faints mercifully against the tortured irresistible sensation at her throat. Dracula drinks and his eyes glow red, his mind intently engaged in piercing the subconscious of his subject, implanting his own unassailable thoughts amid the innermost recesses of her being and thereby protecting them within the neural network of the young girl's brain.)

5

The next evening finds Dracula at the kitchen table discussing the matters of the previous night with Renfield who has been apprehensively skulking about the room.

Dracula - Well Renfield, your friend, I believe you called her Lura... should be fully recovered in a day or two. I'm sorry I bit her in my usual way since she is meant for you, but it makes things much easier that way. You my trusty friend are of course the exception requiring neither bite nor mental coercion, but you are of a rare breed, are you not Renfield?

Renfield - If you say so, master. I remember you once told me that I'm fortunate, because I don't know enough to be afraid. Even after all these years I know you are not a monster even if you have that kind of appearance at times.

Dracula - Yes but someday soon it may be popular to be a monster and then I won't forget your service, or should I say well intentioned activities?

Renfield - Thank you master, I know it's not much... a child here, a rodent there... but I try my best and now with Lura, I should have much more time for your errands. And you've commanded her to stay here at this house when she can so I'll be here too and sometimes even the same room and then maybe even touching... I might go up to her and... (Renfield puts his arms out in front of him as if to reach the object of his dreams while his body jerks in awkward spasms, a parody of joy.) It's unbelievable master, isn't it?

Dracula - (shaking his head) Yes in a way, I suppose it is. In any case when she awakes she will be under your control responding to your simplest wish. So wish wisely because she still has her own ability to think and over time you may lose this control if you use too much force at first. Just be patient and she should be as good a friend, even a lover, as you've ever had. (Renfield's focus shifts to the doorway and the room where Lura rests, a look of rapt nervous expectation written on his features.) Patience Renfield! (Dracula snaps his fingers loudly.) Remember it is she who has been hypnotized, not you...

Renfield - Yes master, will you be hypnotizing others as well? Could you have the movie people vote you an 'Oscar Meyer' award if that is what you want?

Dracula - Don't try me, it is simply the 'Oscar.' Any pork prizes should go to you and your captured ground hog. As for hypnotics, I am a vampire first, not a ruler of zombies. Though hypnosis is convenient on occasion I would like to seek my fame on merit. After all through the centuries I've developed the consummate skills of a master storyteller and actor as was necessary to survive. Mind control is really quite similar to physical force and is used with discretion or a last resort as in finding you a friend! (He laughs.) Just kidding Renfield, but as you might compare the style of an action hero to the diverse talents of a well rounded actor such as Dustin Hoffman or Jack Nickelson, the multifaceted actor's appeal should prevail...

Renfield - I love how Indiana Jones battles the giant spiders, or the Crocodile Dundee, and the way the Schwarzenegger splatters his enemies to bits with his powerful weapons which are still no match for his bulging arms. And I have also fallen in love with that Catwoman from the 'Batman' movies. I wouldn't thank you enough if you could let me meet her though I'm not sure who she might really be!

Dracula - You are an obvious victim, Renfield. But I suppose it wouldn't be good to neglect the action roles too much. That was apparently the mold of my debut film... I'll have to work it out with the production people or maybe an agent... Behave yourself as I must visit the studios tonight and see what the production companies have designed for my next movie. (Dracula departs.)

Renfield - Good luck master, and thank you ever so much!

6

Dracula is whisking through the night air as the words leave Renfield's mouth. Renfield then proceeds to the first floor guest room where Lura lay recovering from the shock of hypnosis and mild blood loss. Renfield has painstakingly arranged colorful yet old-styled woman's clothing which he had come across stored in the attic. The material was an elegant fabric, rich in pattern and texture. He reasoned that if somehow she decided to adorn herself with his selection this then might symbolize her acceptance of him as a friend. Gazing at her attractive figure in shorts and buttoned down cotton blouse he wonders if he should suggest this to her when she awakes or wait to see if she might want to wear his choice on her own. He decides on the later approach so as not to miss the chance of spying undetected while she changes clothes.

Caught up in the excitement of the moment he has the brave idea to begin the process himself and see if he can replace her shirt with his elaborate choice while she sleeps. Quickly, he nimbly tries to fidget with her blouse buttons and turning her slightly manages to remove the item. As he does so however her slight frame shifts enough so that her nearby shapely breast rolls from its loosely fitting undergarment and on to the top of his hand. He shrieks briefly and in a burst of nervous frenzy hurries away from the scene of his making, leaving the young girl to wonder at her position of lewd repose when she wakes up.

A short while later Renfield manages to overcome his inhibitions and worry long enough to gaze in to the room a couple times more and marvel at the beautiful creature who might become his friend. As of yet he still can hardly conceive of it, as Dracula has been his only companion these many years. It is his fortune and destiny to serve the master... a family heritage spanning countless centuries. In fact most civilizations could not boast such a bond with time. With such a strong tradition he often wonders why no one else seems to be aware of it... but that is the way of the master, or at least always has been until this new idea to become a star. Renfield wonders what his father would say. His is a relationship born of convenience and a mutual need for protection from vulnerabilities, imagined and real... the word of Dracula is law. He listens hard in the cold stillness as if to hear his father. And finally decides that he might also say it is an arcane and one sided law at times, but law nevertheless.

As Renfield looks in on Lura the thought of a girlfriend is tempting to his unhinged mind, why this may even help him to regain his sanity! But the thought is fleeting and he finds himself lured back to the kitchen and the enchanting aroma of marinated and sautéed salamanders topped with crispy wolf spiders, he'd been saving them for just such an occasion. He reminds himself to be sure master doesn't want any blood from the groundhog before returning it to its den, to be on the safe side... Actually though he'd been relieved to hear master didn't relish the animal as unearthing the wilily brute had been quite a chore. He wouldn't want to have to make it a regular activity...

7

Dracula sights the hub of several large outdoor movie sets from against the city's dark blue skyline and begins a swooping arcing descent characteristic of bat flight. He lands near the entrance and checks the name, 'Megalithic Film Studios,' to be sure it is not some wealthy resident's private amusement park. He is reassured as Megalithic was the first to place a bid for his movie contract. Money of course was not the crucial issue but he couldn't help appreciate their timely recognition of his talents... Similar to the stars, the immortal vampire has his ego to consider above all else.

Before entering the sprawling real estate of the movie company, he spies a newspaper machine. A front page story catches his attention and he is soon reading about a recent medical research marvel, how a Japanese firm has developed electronic components small enough to be injected in the human blood stream to aid in fighting disease and cancer. He cringes at the thought of ingesting such artificial additives with a meal and realizes that now is the time to gain a more powerful hold on modern society before these medical researchers really go to far... He has often pondered what method or manner the first man made immortality would take. The subject always left him dreading his own vulnerabilities, the light of day, the attack of religious zealots, a stake to the chest... What if these things meant nothing to the new breed of immortal?

He approaches the gate of Megalithic, and its brightly painted barricades and tire shredding devices. A guard jumps to his feet from behind a desk. Recognizing Dracula's characteristic dress from pictures circulated through the company's offices and lobby displays, the guard admits him without question.

Guard - Mr. Dracula, good to see you! I should have known I'd be the likely one to see you, working the night shift! (He laughs at his joke.)

Dracula - I'm impressed that you know me already sir, flattered really. I think I'm going to like this kind of work... and just wanted to take a look at a few of the new sets, you know for ideas, that sort of thing.

The Reemergence of Vlad!

Guard - Sure, anything you say. I'm going to see your movie, the one you did with Brazen Gillpuppy, the first chance I get. I've really got it for her, I hope you don't mind me saying. I guess you do too from the gossip pages. (Dracula thanks him and begins to wander off.) Don't worry, my lips are sealed! (The guard shouts after him.)

Dracula – (muttering) Well your neck may not be before long... (The guard strikes him as rather too talkative for his liking and decides that a reliable cure is in order. First though he'd like to see how the world renowned Hollywood sets appear behind the scenes. He is amused by his pun, *behind the scenes of the scenes...* and soon finds most of the observable sets to be hardly recognizable, being in various phases of construction and so inquires of a casually dressed gentleman he notices to be idling aimlessly about.)

Gentleman - (talking to himself) What do they know? What do any of them know? Who do they think they are? They don't know what they're doing, and who do they blame? Who do they blame when they don't know what they're doing? That's right, me! The one person who really doesn't know. How am I supposed to know what they're doing?! (He turns to address his last question at Dracula and his eyes light with hope.) It's you! You're really here! You are him, aren't you?

Dracula - Good evening... (He utters, bemused with such instant recognition.)

Gentleman - Hi, I'm Sydney Hardgrave, one of the directors on your next picture. My name's not important of course. But you may want to remember who helped you become a big star. (He laughs.) Just kidding, but stranger things have happened, and judging from your obvious appearance will no doubt continue to happen. (Sydney reaches for Dracula's icy handshake and finds it to be a leaden weight.)

Dracula - Excuse me. (smiling) I'm not yet in the habit... (meaning that he does not usually make physical contact unless about to vampirize a victim...)

Sydney - Your fans have been screaming for you and we'd thought we'd lost contact. (He places his hand on Dracula's cape and back, but immediately withdraws it noticing the strange sensation of chiseled ice cold marble.) Yes the production bosses want to get right to work on some scripts. That's right, they already consider your ideas so important, they want your input on the big decisions... probably something to do with how you read your character. You know, the realism. Or perhaps it's in your contract. I don't know. Who am I to know? I'm just glad you're here! (While they walk Sydney explains that the sets, especially the ones outside, are in a constant state of flux, some are being taken apart, others built up... recycling as much as possible.) People have got this idea that there's money to do whatever we want, but there are costs. Let me tell you there are costs! There wouldn't be so many minimum wage jobs in this business if there weren't so many costs. On the plus side big companies are always trying to pay us to do some subliminal advertising, little things during a movie that will advertise a product... things that don't seem like an obvious commercial or maybe they do! But usually that stuff gets in and we don't get paid. On the other hand our stars are the best endorsements. They make money by selling the film itself! And a star can get to the point where he or she generates profits regardless of whether they put out a good or bad image. The lines blur and who wants a good role model these days anyway?

The Reemergence of Vlad!

Though the O.J. thing was extreme, wasn't it? Just about everyone agrees on that, but what if he's innocent? He's got rights, doesn't he? Who better to exercise his rights than a major star, I ask you?

Dracula - Yes, an unfortunate case, but apparently profitable for the news channels.

Sydney - Exactly!

Dracula - Two victims at once, wasn't it... a challenge, even for a vampire...

Sydney - Er, yes. Well if you've seen enough out here, I've got to get going... By the way your sets will be filmed at night I imagine. Anyway now that I've got you, I'd like to invite you to the preproduction party at our producer's house... I'm sure you've heard of him. 'Name starts with 'Spiel' ends with 'berg'... 'Just a couple nights from today and at his private estate. Let me tell you *people* will be there. It'll give you a chance to meet our stars and your co-stars right away. Here's the information. (He hands Dracula a card.) Again, it'll be at night as you might prefer so I hope it won't be a problem. With events like this, there just can't be problems... I'm sure you understand Mr. Dracula? Or is it Count?

Dracula - No, I understand. I should be there. Sounds as if it has all the importance of a mafia family reunion, only with the good guys instead, I'd wager.

Sydney - That would be a good bet, and I'll be there. You may not notice me. You'll have plenty of distractions though, but if you'd like introductions or anything, just name it. Just don't make me a vampire, at least while I still have a 'life!' Ha, just kidding, I've never had a life. I can count on you then! See you. (Sydney Hard-grave scurries off to the conglomerate of offices at the center of the maze of the huge building complex, and discards a wrapper to a roll of antacid tablets along the way.)

8

Dracula decides to take his leave after observing a few more sets including some of the more permanent ones indoor and seeing not much of interest. Maybe the magic of Hollywood is more a factor than he assumed judging from what he would have to work with at the sets... a few mock Gothic buildings, a subterranean waterway, a model of a giant ape and some warehouses. On the plus side he did find a sort of cemetery, but certainly much too small for what he'd be capable of. And most depressing of all... absolutely no sign of a huge stone castle or craggy mountaintop that might portray his ancestral home.

He reaches the guardhouse and remembering his earlier annoyance, sates himself briefly on the sleeping guard's jugular and the mildly alcoholic blood. He notices a small portable TV still on and takes it with him, thus adding a more probable cause for the attack.

9

Dracula arrives home and finds Renfield fussing over an animated groundhog that has been trussed up and placed on a large platter on the kitchen table.

Renfield - Hello master, I wanted to be sure you weren't hungry tonight. It wouldn't be any trouble for me to keep him a few more days. I tried to tame him with some vegetables from the market. Still the way he squirms, he may last a few more days...

Dracula - No thank you Renfield, please put him out. I can't relax with that constant snorting.

Renfield - I could put him back in the... (Dracula sternly points toward the front door, his facial features grim and serious. Renfield carries the pig to the front door and releases its bindings, sending it galloping off into the darkness.) It is done master. I know you'd prefer Lura and I understand if you must kill her. But I hope you let me keep her a while longer... She did not run from me immediately as many people, especially women, do. And she seems willing to accept anything I ask of her now. But I only asked that she come to our house a couple hours a day or whenever she isn't busy with her usual life so that people will not become suspicious. She obeyed as you promised she would... Your bite is very strong, master, I'm sure you will have no problems in Hollywood! Maybe you can teach me someday... (Renfield makes feeble snarling gestures.) Maybe then I could have bitten the groundhog! (Renfield shakes his head from side to side baring his unsightly teeth while pretending to be a savage animal.)

Dracula - Please Renfield, I have a headache. Don't worry about your girlfriend, I have no need of her. I've dined again this evening, three times in as many nights! Just recently, a security guard, and while hardly enjoyable, a meal nonetheless. I've also brought something you might put to some use. (Dracula alerts Renfield to the presence of the TV he has placed on the counter top in the darkened room.) It is a common television, but runs on batteries so that you might enjoy it without the troubles of electric service.

Renfield - Thank you master.

Dracula - You might learn some new recipes if you watch the channels with the cooking shows.

Renfield - That would be wonderful.

Dracula - I'm sure anything would be an improvement.

Renfield - I'm sorry. Master, I was wondering if you ever miss the taste of the other food... you know what the others eat. It seems you might not prefer the things I prepare for myself, spiders and such. But maybe Lura could... and I can try with the television also to find something, a nice slimy okra and wormwood pie for instance or gourmet frog's legs and crunchy sand crabs... even a feast of blood rare meat? Doesn't that sound delicious? (Dracula frowns.) And you might want to get in the practice of eating anyway when you are with your Hollywood friends. What if they want you to go with them for dining?

Dracula - I'm glad you're so concerned, my faithful Renfield. However I doubt they will be so insistent as to demand that I eat in their presence. Though they may think me odd if at a formal dinner they are all relishing the same food, but that might only happen at some club or cult gathering. The movie people of Hollywood will certainly have diverse tastes as I'm sure there must be many eccentric types and unusual personalities among them. Just the same, you are probably right. I remember once I had to eat an entire rack of ram ribs in order to prove my strength and worth as a man to a group of mountain villagers, gaining their trust to later attack their women with abandon. An ordeal it was, but fortunately not the sort of thing that requisites practice. No I rather think my new friends will be more interested to try my diet than I, theirs. After all what celebrity wouldn't want real immortality? I'll be simply there, giving them what they want.

Renfield - Yes master, did you start working on your next movie tonight?

Dracula - Not quite yet, I'll first be attending a party at the residence of the producer fellow, this Spielberg. So I will be in my coffin until then resting. I'll have to be at my best for my first meeting with my bosses. I can hardly believe what I hear myself saying... (as he turns to depart) the indignity of it! I suppose it might not be that bad. They may even be entertaining, these *bosses*! They no doubt expect the same of me. I expect they'll see that Count Dracula will have no trouble on his side of that bargain! (He says as he trips on a loose board at the top of the stairs to find himself again lying amidst a rising cloud of dust and cellar soot.)

Renfield - (calling downstairs) Shall I wake you in two days then, master?

Dracula - Yes Renfield. (then quietly) If you haven't already destroyed me by then... with your wretchedness, you spurious scoundrel and craver of crawling things! (Once more in his coffin, Dracula finds solace in the earth, and a state of immortal trance-like repose instantly envelopes him.)

10

Days later, Dracula awakes to the sound of Renfield tapping on his coffin...

Renfield - It is time for you to go to Hollywood... You asked that I...

Dracula - (raspingly) Yes Renfield! Yesss. (The lid slides back slowly with a creak.)

Renfield - (backing away) I hope you like the new stairway. I made it myself... to save money and keep them away. You know those workmen with their big hammers and the pounding. They might want to drive a stake... (Renfield notices that due to the prolonged rest, Dracula had become almost completely submerged beneath the loamy soil and now exits the casket as some slinking reptile or amphibian might emerge from its underground burrow. Renfield is fascinated by the motions but quickly retreats upstairs seeing his master assume his formidable caped form. When Dracula appears upstairs near the kitchen Renfield addresses him...) Master, before you go. I was wondering if you might like to try a new style of dress... In the attic I uncovered a nice new suit that may be your size... a little off-black though. Is gray alright?

Dracula - I don't think so, though I suppose a fresh shirt couldn't hurt.

The Reemergence of Vlad!

(Renfield hands him a white shirt, embroidered and with ruffles at the edges. Dracula notices the scent.) Ah, preserved in cedar. I should have a guest casket made from that wood sometime, perhaps several.

Renfield - Yes master. (He still holds out a suit for Dracula's inspection.)

Dracula - And considering the occasion I guess you can rinse out my cape, which should dry sufficiently in flight tonight. (Dracula hands over a slightly rumpled somewhat musty cape, remarkably resilient to the touch, shiny and black.) You know I've had this same suit some two hundred years without cause for replacement. And though you wouldn't know it, the fabric has been rent on numerous excursions... I like its plain style and its constant proximity to my form lends it a certain enduring character of its own. (Receiving the garment, Renfield immediately sets upon his task, vigorously scrubbing at the kitchen sink.) Actually this cloth (considering Renfield's replacement shirt) is modeled after an older French cut, early seventeenth century, I believe. So this might be better termed, old fashioned, or out-of-style. It is of no great importance... I'll wear it because it's fresh and it amuses me. Thank you Renfield. (Renfield returns the cape.)

Renfield - Have a good time master, I'm sure you're on your way to becoming a big star!

11

Dracula, now dripping wet, strides through the house and out into the night air. Checking his map against the directions he folds them back in his cape which immediately melds into the webbing of his huge wings and he takes to the sky. He is soon surprised to recognize the familiarity of the terrain with tall sculpted shrubberies, imposing against the skyline as Romanesque columns. Suddenly he is reminded that he has already visited this same property several nights earlier when he had encountered an attractive young girl at poolside. The realization dawns on him that the girl had indeed used the name, Spielberg... Darla Spiel-berg. Oh well, he would have to be prepared to call on his powers of concentration and tact at a moment's notice.

This time he alights near the front entrance and at a moderate distance so as not to be careless or appear too obvious a curiosity. Many guests have already arrived and as he walks quickly to the door he is met by another coming along a different path.

Guest - Hi there, Mr. ...

Dracula - Dracula.

Guest - Oh, of course. Scorsese here, or Marty if you'd like... Well it's a great night isn't it... bright moon, (he stares at Dracula briefly) just the night for your sort of thing, (He pauses.) You know, you're probably going to say I'm crazy but I could have sworn I just saw you flying a moment ago!

The Reemergence of Vlad!

Dracula – (extending his hand in greeting) Yes, at night... sometimes one sees strange things. I have a habit of walking fast and my cape sometimes catches the breeze.

Scorsese - (returning the handshake) I guess that's it. Or maybe your shadow against the side of the white mansion. Ever notice that, how shadows seem to fly by when you're at the right angle to the light?

Dracula - An intriguing observation! (Dracula watches his expression for any indication of undo alarm or surprise but notes only a look of cautious curiosity. They reach the door and Dracula hesitates a moment, not sure that the man would immediately reveal to everyone what he saw or whether the explanations had convinced him.)

They enter through a well-lit foyer and see many guests ambling about wearing diverse fashions. Dracula is relieved that Scorsese has not run off in one direction or other to report their unusual meeting. Dracula's cape is still damp from its washing and begins reacting to the light. A mist-like vapor quickly envelops him that resembles a small cloud formation. Some guests appear startled.

Woman - (talking with acquaintance) It's not a fire, is it?

Other Woman - No, I don't think so. Say, it might be that Dracula fellow. That's who it looked like when he came in. I heard he's the guest of honor, recently signed on with the studio or so I've heard, though I wouldn't know definitely. Who has time to keep up with all the reasons for every party!

First Woman - Do you think he's alright?

12

A friend standing next to Mr. Spielberg and overhearing the women...

Friend - (to Spielberg) He's okay. He's got a real assortment of stunts and tricks. He used some on the last movie: hypnotics, sleight-of-hand, fooling mirrors... that sort of thing. I'll call him over. (louder) Dracula, over here please. (Dracula comes over along with his trailing vapor cloud. Spielberg's friend makes some polite introductions.)

Dracula - Thank you for the invitation. Please excuse my cape, it is made from a light sensitive material.

Spielberg - Very interesting Vlad. May I call you Vlad? I know you hadn't mentioned it, but that would of course be the first name of the historic Dracula... wouldn't it?

Dracula - No I don't mind... He says as young girls arrive at his side to take his cape. The name of course but I'd prefer to keep my... The eager young girls have already made off with his smoking outer garment and the attached bloodstone neck clasp. He makes an effort to snatch the stone but the giggling girls have already gone.

Spielberg - Don't worry, we'll do what we can to keep the myth alive. I guess the best way to get started would be a toast! (Raising his voice and motioning...) Blood for everyone! (Large trays of glasses containing a red liquid are set out for the party goers. When they pick up the glasses they notice them to be throbbing slightly as a result of some unseen mechanical device inserted at the base of each glass. Dracula is at first enchanted and then disappointed somewhat to realize that the liquid which has a smooth texture and the thickness of blood is in reality a kind of alcoholic and fruit concoction.) Let's drink a toast with a drink that can stop your heart in honor of our new guest and honored star, Dracula! (cheers) And when the beating stops you'll know you've killed your drink! (The guests laugh and drink except for Dracula. Spielberg notices and looks concerned.) I hope you don't think the joke's in poor taste, Vlad.

Dracula - No, I wouldn't say that. Although I do think I'm not completely devoid of morals... I apologize, a word mired with religious overtones. I'm just not in the habit of killing my victims you understand, most are real people after all but perhaps this once considering it is just a glass! (He laughs.)

Spielberg - Very admirable... I'll have to take that into account with the script department. That always seems to be the priority of the biggest stars, not to look one sided, or devoid of dimension... I can see you're not about to let yourself be exploited and don't worry we'll try to hash out the religious angles as well. Full script approval... star privilege Vlad, at no charge! (He laughs.) Well I'll let you meet your new friends now. I don't need to remind you there are a number of actresses in attendance who are unfettered romantically, or so say the tabloids. Time to have a good time, but let's not play too rough. (He smiles to show some teeth, claps Dracula's shoulder and departs.)

13

Dracula enters the throng of the party and is soon awash in introductions, questions and glad salutations. He is surprised by the pointedness and alarming candidness of the remarks he hears but is appeased by further rounds of handshakes and toasts. As he turns away from the main crowd of guests he is shocked to notice two of his personal favorite female stars standing together a short distance from him. He hastily approaches.

Dracula - Excuse me. Forgive the intrusion, but I couldn't help recognize two of the celebrities I'd most hoped most to meet. (He smiles inadvertently exposing his canines but employs a disarming expression with genuine appreciation for their presence.) You are celebrities aren't you? (He smiles again hoping to cover his obvious gaffe.)

Madonna - Hello Count. I know you're new to Hollywood, so you're probably just trying to flatter us. But trying and *doing* are different things aren't they? (she laughs) My name's Madonna and this is Christina Applegate.

Dracula - Yes, of course. It's true I am not too familiar with the entertainment world yet. I've only recently acquired a television, but I try to keep abreast... stay current... reading newspapers, the dreadful rumor magazines and the movies of course, some movies... It was when I noticed the lovely Kelly Bundy and her endearing television friends and family that I knew I would have to have one, a TV set that is... In truth I'd become a regular bar patron just so I might watch her show, for the reruns at night of course.

Christina - That's sweet.

Madonna - Yeah great. You know you look a little different without your cape, but don't worry the media probably isn't here yet so your image is still safe. (She laughs again.) So... (after pausing to notice his distraction with Christina) what do you hate about Hollywood so far?

Dracula - There are usually plenty of things bothering me. But I'm afraid I just haven't been here long enough. Though just recently I was asked by someone... it's such a nice change of pace this recognition by fans as opposed to... well let's leave the topic of victims for a more suitable moment, ha. Anyway this young tempting girl, a fan of mine I met a bar that caters to vampires wanted to know if my name really meant 'devil' or 'dragon' and how I managed to escape all the stakings and beheadings at my castle during the fifteenth century! I agreed they were important historical points and like that fanatical book, the Bible, seem to have inherent contradictions, but I am not at all used to talking of those things in public... even among vampires...

Madonna – Well who could blame you! (laughing) But that's horrible Count! You'll see that Hollywood is worse than anywhere else. The media can turn up anywhere you know, and it's hard to know who to trust! (She says while rubbing her neck protectively.) And if they can't find you, they'll just make something up. With me, I was just telling Christy... my recent bitch (she smiles deceptively, Christina looks skyward) I mean *complaint*, is this the new thing with skin magazines, when they print these horribly fictitious erotic stories about celebrities. Why can't they go with the facts! I mean there are plenty of juicy facts and certainly enough to go around if you know where to look...

What was the name of that bar by the way, I haven't really tried the vampire scene yet. I'm dying to sometime at least try the look, not the lifestyle though, too confining with the coffins and all. (She coughs and giggles.) 'Anyway getting back to our little beef, excuse the pun (winks at Christina and giggles again) but well you can't help but read some of tawdry rags and what they come up with is... I don't really know you good enough yet to say. Maybe in a couple minutes! (she laughs) Just write down your address... (She holds up her arm for Vlad to write on.)

Christina - Just see for yourself Mr. Count, everybody's reading them! (She smiles at Madonna and glances at her near total cleavage.)

Dracula - I suppose I will. (prying his eyes away from Madonna's arm and breast) I haven't been keeping up with the latest in erotic literature. Judging from Madonna's music videos I realize what an important area of concern that must be for her... being so involved, with all of that! (He grasps her arm firmly and with his other hand uses his sharpened finger nails to write in small hasty letters a bit of information there.)

Madonna – (looking startled but not wincing) A star has an obligation to her fans as I'm sure you'll realize one day. (retrieving her arm and again laughing while also staring) You'll have to excuse me Count, besides I know you want to talk to Christina alone. But just one thing... We couldn't help notice that trick you did with your cape, were you trying to breath fire or something? Or did someone light you up accidentally? (She gazes down at her forearm and squints at the writing.) And what's your stance on garlic pizza? (She pats his midriff.) Kidding, but maybe you'll let me find out sometime! (She smiles, pleased with the effect of her words and walks away.)

The Reemergence of Vlad!

Dracula - (to Christina) I guess her problem is one of exploitation, something all stars probably struggle with. And I can commiserate for with me the problem has probably existed a lot longer... (He fixes an hypnotic look on her but she gazes away and sips her drink.) Fortunately I would doubt that you, much like the free spirited Kelly Bundy or Jessie was it, should have any care in life or at least I hope not. Maybe you could tell me what you fear instead? (He muses, revealing his ample gleaming incisors.)

Christina - Well, namely just the normal fears like spiders falling down on you or even bats you know with that crazy way they fly... swooping and diving. I suppose a real vampire attack might be the worst thing if they existed... (glancing at Dracula) but the others are bad enough, you know from the older producers or directors and all that power they have at the studio, except for Mr. Spielberg of course! You'd be surprised how many vampires there are. They'll probably come out of the closet now that you're here. (She laughs.)

Dracula - I can imagine how an under aged actress, actresses such as yourself hold a fascination for certain types of men... (He again tries unsuccessfully to hypnotize her.)

Christina - Hmmm, I'm not under aged anymore but I'm still afraid of bats and spiders. In fact, when the writers found out at 'Married,' they gave my character a job as a 'Verminator' where I did a series of commercials about pest control. Oh or I suppose those phobias could have started after I did the Verminator, I was just a kid back then you know. That's already ancient history, ha, relatively for a normal human that is.

Dracula - Amusing. I'll have to see to it that if you ever accept an invitation to visit, my housekeeper will be confined to his quarters. Rather than trying to control the insects he has a very real habit of cultivating them... First things first, you will accept won't you? (He smiles showing more tooth than necessary, but trying not to lose control...)

Christina - Oh.

Dracula - Needless to say, I've located his rooms far from the main parts of the house. (He begins to noticeably salivate while he considers his prize.)

Christina – (glancing about) I think that some of your producers and directors are looking over here. They may want to talk with you... (She starts to leave and Dracula suggests maybe they'll do a movie together, and that he'll refrain from forming into a bat in her presence... if that would please her. She summons a smile for his bizarre charm.) Eternal life might be interesting for a while! (She likes his stark features but has noticed his animalistic teeth and eyes tinged red... slightly glowing. She snugs her arms close to her waist.)

Dracula - That could easily be arranged upon your visit! (He catches her eyes briefly and hands her an engraved card which she snatches quickly keeping her arms out of harms way.) But then you already know my address don't you?

Christina – (pausing then checking the card) Yes, but how did you, I mean, how do I know that? (Immediately the card disintegrates to ash...) Thanks for the offer, (says while backing up) I'll consider it... (She hurries away checking frequently over her shoulder and thankful her arm was not utilized for the stunt.)

14

A man comes up to Dracula introducing himself as Cal, one of his producers...

Cal - That's what I like to see, not wasting any time hobnobbing with the highest paid vixens. Star or no, they've got their buttons like the rest of us, eh? Did you get her number? (He smiles. Dracula regards him casually.)

Dracula - I've admired her for some time. We happened to be discussing her fears which frightened her I suppose.

Cal - There's certainly plenty to be frightened about in this business! People will try to tell you for example that you've started too late... won't last, too old... that sort of thing.

Dracula - I'm sure you would not want to comprehend my true age.

Cal - That may be but don't let it bother you. You've still got good skin and the studio believes in you, that's what matters... (then to himself) although how they decide these things is anybody's guess. (to Dracula) But in all sincerity, the skin looks good, a little pale perhaps but durable. Reminds me a bit of the conditioned look of a Liz Taylor or Cher dermis, topnotch really... the sky's the limit.

There is one thing that's got me a little concerned though. There was a report from security over at the studio... Well the gist of it was something about you believing you're a vampire or if you'd hear them tell it, might actually

81

be one. Seems a guard claims to have been bitten on the neck. I wouldn't worry too much, he was probably found sleeping and then concocted a story. We had to let him go.

Dracula - That is unfortunate.

Cal - The studio backs its stars. Anyway, regarding fears, probably the most pervasive one in Hollywood is the inevitability of aging. It's a safe bet that most stars would give anything to be real life vampires. Why most of them look the part so why not take it one step further and go the full nine yards, or give them the enchilada if you will?

Dracula - Indeed. (He says, shifting his eyes from side to side wondering at his point.)

Cal - If you've got a minute, I can tell you from experience what makes this place tick. (He downs a large part of his drink. Dracula nods.) Though aging is normal and it's natural to fear it, there's one thing no one wants, and that's a dead career! To a celebrity there's nothing worse, no matter what the age! (he laughs) It can be as traumatic as the real thing, death I mean, to a major name. (he says with a lowered voice)

Dracula - A depressing topic, but a human concern I imagine. And one which I hope to address on screen... fear for actual rather than perceived 'death' that is.

Cal - Exactly. It's a hot topic and getting hotter. We need someone with your style, a Dracula so to speak, to handle it. Death, a hot topic... only in Hollywood! (coughs)

Dracula - I feel qualified and will do my best, don't worry.

Cal - There you are! With all the mania these days for youth-maintenance and recycled bodies, you can't miss. The entertainment community at large is responsible for half the snake oil products out there. You can be assured that most of the vitamin creams, Chinese herbals and ground shark cartilages produced are shipped straight into celebrity homes. Of course your natural diets and exercise programs get a lot of attention. Sure it's depressing, I just want to let you know you've got your work cut out. (The producer takes a closer look at Dracula's bloodless features and suggests...) I've heard rare meat and vitamins once in a while though is good for that sallow look. And B-12 might do something for the blood.

Dracula - Yes I know.

Cal - Of course you do... now I'm doing it! (He laughs a little then displays an expression of concern that fades to confusion before continuing... Dracula feels the conversation has grown tiresome and hypnotically befuddles him with a cryptic stare.) Funny I was trying to say... that you're invited to our offices tomorrow for the meeting on project ideas... that would be tomorrow evening. (He suddenly finds words that seem to project themselves forward somehow, assuming a dire importance in his mind and necessitating utterance even though he knows the meeting is actually scheduled for the late afternoon. Changes will have to be made he realizes.) Thank you then for your considerate and er... considerable attention. I look forward to working with you and will keep your wishes in mind. Goodnight Vlad. (He walks away wondering about the strange certainty of Dracula's wishes but knowing that the Count hadn't actually *said* anything about them.)

15

The evening has taken on a more subdued tone, the lights are lower, the music less distracting... Dracula takes the opportunity to eavesdrop on the various discussions going on around him.)

Studio Accountant - Do you realize what these vampire movies cost? The lighting requirements, special film, eccentric stars... Did you get a look at our Dracula? Is that aura or what? You can tell if a picture's going over budget by looking at the star!

Other Accountant - True... True...

(Then a more distant conversation...)

Special Effects Technician - Did you hear they'll be playing up the angle of immortality heavy on this one. They're bringing in medical experts from all over. I was just talking to one, he told me there's a lot more to the aging process than the buildup of waste products in the cells and fat inside the arteries... that the chromosomes actually make some hormone that causes your body to start aging.

Other Technician - Hey let's keep my body out of it! (laughing...)

First Technician - No really, it starts happening while you're still growing...

Other Technician - Well thank God for that, I stopped growing in my teens!

The Reemergence of Vlad!

First Technician - Jeez you must be looped... Listen, it's when you've grown that the hormone ramps up production and that's why you're getting more mortal all the time.

Other Technician - Oh so you're saying that with a little chemical alteration we could live like kids forever? That makes sense. You know maybe we should just die when we're still kids, after all if you're going to be a kid your whole life what's the use!

First Technician - I give up. What're you drinking anyway? (He checks the other's glass.)

(Dracula is suddenly distracted tuning his ears and hearing Christina Applegate, sounding every bit like Kelly Bundy, in conversation with Darla Spielberg and several young men out on the terrace. He is plagued by the impulse to implant thoughts of desire and allegiance but remembers the results produced with his first picture's co-star, Brazen Gillpuppy. No, he would have to be more tactful selecting his willing mistress... It wouldn't do to be arrested again for biting an actress. Judging from her allure though and that of some of the other female guests in attendance, a quick meal may be well worth the risk at that. As he is about to reach a decision, his concentration is again sidetracked by a perspiring short man he remembers meeting during his visit to the studio lots.)

Sydney Hardgrave - Hi, Sydney here or director Hardgrave, whatever you prefer. And as I always say, it's not whatever or whichever you say but how you say it or however! So how are you Vlad? (barely pausing) The company just wanted me to talk with you about one more thing... You've probably been fed the rumors of what we pay our people so before you get too jealous of other star salaries, remember you're still new. And you're under contract regardless. (He laughs briefly.) But just to give you advance warning if you haven't suspected it already, most big stars are spoiled babies, plain and simple... they see what the next one's are making and they want more. Once you get sucked into the vacuum of box office sensation, there's no turning back. You run on pure ego. Why your fans demand it! There's no way you can refuse it; you command the premium and the premium is image. We all know that image is what... (without waiting for a reply) everything in this business! And unfortunately it doesn't come cheap. Somebody has to pay for that image and that's what we, those of us in the trenches at the production company do! That's our job and when you see the offices you'll know what I mean by *trenches*. And incredibly work gets done there. So that's it... in a nutshell. (He appears mildly pleased with himself and blissfully looks about.) You'll excuse me won't you now Vlad, I think I see another star, this one a lady that needs talking to... (He walks away winking, apparently unaware he has held an entire conversation with himself, as is often the case with hypertensive types. Dracula scowls at the blueprint laid before him like so many hors d'oeuvres at a party. And like the fancy food morsels, Dracula decides he has had enough processing for one night and with polite greetings along the way retrieves his cape and departs the mansion.)

16

The next evening Dracula arrives at the studios and is allowed access to the script meetings as stipulated in his contract. Unfortunately he neglected to insist on controlling the time they might meet in writing and his hypnosis of one of the scriptwriters has only caused a delay, which at least prolongs the meeting till after dark. The result is that he has missed most of the decisions reached on plot considerations. The movie outline has undergone many revisions, and now finalized it is presented to Dracula for approval. He learns the setting takes place at a point in the near future where humans may no longer exist, just android and cyborg-like creatures that are the immortal remnants of the human race and of course there are some vampire survivors... Vampires though dominating the world briefly during the initial conflict between humans and cyborgs, have now been declining in numbers since the proliferation of the cyborgs.

Clearly superior due to their lack of vulnerabilities and awesome capabilities the cyborgs are now to vampires what the vampires were to humans... In fact it seems that owing to their past history of conquest over humankind vampires are routinely killed for sport. New technologies allow for the instant identification of the vampire trait. Vampires now also no longer have a reliable food source in terms of human blood and so have been reduced to scavenging animals for their survival.

A hundred years prior to this though vampires had held almost godlike dominion, herding vast populations of the remaining humans in communities as cattle, where they grouped together for protection much as one might expect to see in a typical B grade zombie movie at the turn of the century... with the exception that vampires possess powers far in excess of that of typical zombies. The human population steadily dwindled while the ranks of vampires (aka zombies) grew... until (much like a movie plot resolution designed to supply a *happy ending*, at the verge of devastation human science manages to perfect the cyborg, the automated man, a being whose thought processes are generated and recorded on computerized hardware and whose body only shares the most rudimentary of similarities with humans, mainly those regarding form and movement! But most amazing of all is that their identity, memory and the way a particular person might think... has been faithfully reproduced. The process of thought in inanimate beings is much more than being manufactured but also accurately transferable from human hosts! (Dracula stops reading. Suddenly agitated and concerned about the horrible and realistic implications the future passage of time presents, humans converting into cyborgs on a massive scale. He can hardly contain his paranoia... as so often has popular science fiction led the way to science fact. Why just consider space travel and the space shuttle, star trek communicators and phasers, and the subsequent development cell phones and tasers. He seethes with almost palpable malevolence for these writers.)

Dracula – (giving voice to his concerns) Of course this might be one outcome... but so incredibly unlikely! How would these strange ideas address the problem of leaving the mortal body behind, or might there be a dual identity until the physical body dies... leaving an encoded cyborg to continue on? And then what of the vampires? Couldn't they transfer identities as well? They would have need if they were truly inferior as you say!

Head Script Writer - (coughing and twirling his pencil) I see the project interests you! Of course you've got to remember... Dracula (then whispering to the fellow next to him...) Is that really his name?

Others - Shhh!

Head Script Writer - (continuing) You've got to remember this is only a movie. I don't think people will be too interested to see both vampires and cyborgs living the *happy ending*! Besides vampires have to pay for decimating the humans in the first place... Vampires will have their moment but ultimately they'll be the bad guys like they always are and will be! Moviewise that is... (He notices Dracula's cruel expression of anger spreading across the *actor's* facial features.)

Others - (general sounds of agreement, some clapping)

2nd Script Writer - And as far as the actual details of transferring identity, the cyborgs could be encoded and then placed in storage until the time they're needed... the circuitry being updated with fresh information continuously.

3rd Script Writer - Not that that would be too critical in most cases... How many people would want to recall their dying days or even the last weeks or even years? Have you ever been to a nursing home... there's not a lot of memorable stuff happening in some cases!

4th Script Writer - One thing we haven't worked out however is the possibility of multiple transference... you know, one human encoding himself into several or even hundreds of cyborgs... 'Could get hairy!

Dracula - It could indeed. (pouting pensively) And obviously a much more pernicious problem than the vampire trait...

5th Script Writer - Yeah and what if one cyborg decides to have all the others erased and encodes himself into all of them? Think about it...

4th Script Writer - I think we probably already have enough to work with just vampires as the bad guys...

Others - (General sounds of agreement as the head script writer signals the end of the meeting and the room empties.)

Dracula - I should bite everyone of them! (thinking out loud and then notices he is alone...) Who finds these writers anyway? From what cemetery are they dug? Maybe the producers can find another set in time. Imagine, treating vampires in such an inconsequential fashion! They should be vampirized but left entombed for eternity for their feeble attempts at writing my script... Maybe I should settle for an epic biography regaling past exploits. No, there will be time for documentaries later.

I'll have to make influential converts soon, and summon the oldest ones with our imminent need to ascend to the rightful cause... no small tasks especially when busily engaged in making movies. The last resort is to of course control as much of the movie making myself as possible in spite of these writers, otherwise my true entity and what I have to offer might never be known! At least some of humanity might be spared their miserable existence if they could only be made to understand... what their accursed future brings! (His eyes flame red as wave after wave of molten heat emanate from his usually icy cold exterior. He dematerializes into a fine mist and seeps out a nearby window into the chill night air.)

17

Dracula decides against maiming the writers for the moment and returns home to find Renfield pacing the hall instead of absorbed in his usual pastimes of cooking or insect watching.

Renfield - Master it is terrible, so terrible what they have done. I tried to stop them... (Dracula notices an unusual odor and sees that Renfield's drab clothing contains splotchy darker areas of a drying liquid.) He had a special name... He said he was the Ex-terminator. I thought he was from the movie with the Schwarzenegger. Maybe you had met him and asked him to visit as a surprise! I was so excited I let him in, and then several more were with him but none of them *him*! And this was worse, so much worse... than any movie. They wanted to kill my insects, and murder them all!

Dracula - So you tried to stop them and they sprayed you by mistake?

Renfield - It was no use... maybe if Lura had been here. They even sprayed downstairs!

Dracula - Don't worry about that, you can get new insects. I don't like bugs downstairs anyway...

Renfield - Yes, but they will die when I bring them inside now. Only some of the rooms that were locked are still safe.

Dracula - Renfield! Stop sniveling, didn't they say anything else... Who sent them?

Renfield - I think they said the payment was a professional curtsy or courtesy, and also that your puddle-cyst or pebble-sis ordered it.

Dracula - Publicist?

Renfield - Maybe. They said he was in charge of important things and that the house should be ready if there might be guests or news cameras... But I don't want the puble-cist coming. He won't like me and then I'll be exterminated!

Dracula - Relax, Renfield... the house will probably have to be professionally cleaned as well, unless you're up to the task. We have to try to put on appearances. If you keep to your room things will be alright. It will be difficult, but I may need to present an image to the light of day.

Renfield - I hope if others come they will be nice... not like today. I couldn't even spare your coffin from the exterminators .

Dracula - Renfield, no! (Dracula descends to his chamber to inspect the damage with Renfield close behind.) The soil has been soaked with poison, Renfield! Maybe it wasn't a good idea to let you have a girlfriend?

Renfield - No master, I tried. I really did. I threw myself...

Dracula - I know. It's probably better to be treated in this casual manner than to be feared as some sort of demon, fiend or devil. That will come later. (He considers the violated earth.) If I remove the top layer and turn the soil a little...

Renfield - I told them I liked the insects and not to bother, but they wouldn't listen. But when they were upstairs I showed them my termite pudding and it was then they left. At least they didn't find my termite nests. I brought them with me on our trip! You don't mind, do you master?

92

The Reemergence of Vlad!

Dracula - It is a gift you know Renfield, to be able to find consolation in such things...

Renfield - Thank you master.

Dracula - Renfield?

Renfield - Yes?

Dracula - Didn't you say earlier that there had been no luggage?

Renfield - None for me, that's right master...

Dracula - And you didn't carry these insects on your person?

Renfield - Oh no... without their wood, termites are very restless. They would have tried to escape and crawl away... (He says while running his finger along the edge of the prodigious casket.)

Dracula glances to one corner where the ancient oak had been crafted into neat seams and sees several pore-like openings and below, a pile of small pasty white insects turning and twisting on the poisoned floor.

Dracula - Renfield, how could you? (Using his pointed almost spike-like nails as prying implements, Dracula causes several large slats to fall away on one side. Renfield's eyes grow wide as they look at extensive networks of tunneling and channels choked with the busy white bodies. Battalions of darker and much larger soldiers, some an inch or more, rush to the exposed surface waving the over-sized pinching jaws on their heads to the open air...)

Renfield - The casket is a little lighter, that is all. I promise master. I was going to move them immediately but there's been so much to do. I will do it now, don't worry!

Dracula - Please Renfield... (climbing upstairs) The new furniture will serve until then; just try and get them all won't you? (then to himself) And I thought a girlfriend somehow... for him.

Renfield carefully studies his hoard as a shepherd might watch a wayward flock.

PART III

THE YOUNG VAMPIRES

Dracula is at a secluded bar in a less popular section of Hollywood. A couple are seated near him. They like his looks and are uninhibited and young.

Guy - Blood?

Dracula - No, Vlad, with a vee.

Guy - Vlod. Oh, too bad it's not Blood. I like that.

Dracula – Yes. (smiles) And you are?

Guy - Just call me Guy, and the girl, Panda... you know, like a Panda Bear. (Dracula apprises her young features.) Would you like to meet my Panda bare? (Dracula nods) Well you can't, she's got clothes on! (he laughs, and she shakes her head... Dracula smiles broadly)

Dracula - I can appreciate a good joke.

Panda - You just need to hear it more often, like every day! (she smiles)

Dracula - It must be nice to see you everyday... clothes or no clothes.

Guy - No clothes is better, usually. (Panda punches him lightly, then whispers something...) She says she likes your clothes. And you're wearing the latest Italian cloak because...

Panda - You're a world acclaimed fashion designer?

Dracula - Sadly the designer passed away some time ago and it is not popular these days, but I may soon be famous for another reason. I'm acting in one of the most important movies about vampires ever made.

Guy - You don't know how long I've waited to meet a star!

Panda - I think he's cute.

Dracula - It's actually a very serious treatment, not a typical Hollywood production.

Guy - Oh, too bad. You can't beat a big FX Hollyweird blockbuster! But it's hard to know what the public wants, you'll probably do okay.

Dracula – It will be big, the bigger the better! What I would like is to be able to hire more extras and actors as vampires. I have some artistic license in the film's production, and must do what I can to save it from the hands of the writers.

Guy - Like I always say, a vampire in need is a friend indeed, just ask Panda. (she hugs Vlad) Come on, I've got vampires for you... Is twenty too many?

Dracula - That's a start. (They walk the streets to a nearby apartment crowded with young people enjoying themselves, each other and their drugs of choice, beer and the sweet smoke of a certain flowering herb. Most are sitting along the walls or lounging in chairs... the air heavy with smoke and seductive

The Reemergence of Vlad!

background music playing.)

Guy - Hey guys! (some return the greeting with, 'Hey Guy,' then some laughter) 'Got someone here who wants to see Panda naked. (Vlad smiles slightly at Panda, she smiles back. Some call out, 'Panda Bear.') There's a man here, name of Vlod.

Panda - Vlad.

Guy - *Vlad*, sorry who's going to put us all in a movie! (shouts of 'alright')

Simone (Punk #1) – (yelling) I wanna be in something with 'Hardcore' in the title.

Guy – (yells back) Hey I know, why don't you act in something that's already been made. (pausing for effect) Listen, he told me on the way over. We're going to be vampires and fight for our immortal lives against cyborg robots. What do you say? (no response) It's got modern day relevance. Things like this are already happening. You've heard of... technology right? You know ipods, PC's, gameboys (winks at Panda), GPS, robots!

Sid (Punk #2) - Yeah free CD's.... I can use 'em! Make sure our robots come with CD drives, righteous!

Pansy (Punk #3) – I wanna be a cyborg! And I want mine to play the Blu Ray discs.

Casey (Punk #4) – My lawyer's gotta see a copy of the script, hah!

Guy - No, we're the vampires! What do you think Fred? Fame! Fortune! We'll be recognized on the street!

Sid – I wanna see Pansy play CD's from her robotic ass. (loud shouts of 'Panda too!')

Kevin (Punk #5) – Hey with my police record I'm already recognized in forty states and most principalities whatever they are, I need to be a robot too! Only metal makeup will do for me! Where's my free CD?? (He holds up a home rolled cigarette before passing out.)

Dave (Punk #6) - Chill punk! My lawyer says I'm already booked but we can do lunch, haah! That's not definite though. (laughs at his joke and snatches Kevin's jay.)

Sid - Sorry Pansy but my contract stipulates that all chicks in my scenes have to be nude... and must report to my trailer after filming!

Pansy - Yea, shut up yer holes, ya dang hairy potters, ya pot holers, ya ... you know what you are don't you? Sid! (voice rising in pitch)

Sid – Someone better take the CD out of Pansy's but or it'll get scratched! (har, har! Pansy fumes)

Fred - Well I personally don't want to get any of that hypnotic crap thrown at me. Vampires always do that shit. Man, you get hypnotized when you're high and that's it. You might never get your mind back man.

Sid - What mind is that Fred? (laughs)

Fred – The one from last semester when I aced that art class...

Guy - What do you say Vlad?

Dracula - Sure you want to be high then the vampire's the thing to be, not a cyborg. Vampires can fly, can't they... just like bats! (Vlad raises his arms and flaps his cloak.)

Fred - Hey man, you're making me dizzy with that.

Kevin – (coming back to life) Me too. And now I'm hypnotized I think, what do I do? Snap me out of it before something weird happens... uh oh I think Pansy's turning into a spank me bitch! Am I right Sid? (He nods, while

The Reemergence of Vlad!

Pansy and Panda display their nails like claws.)

Casey - Hey can you turn into a bat, man?

Pansy - His coat is a bat! Look! (They notice the cape is still lightly flapping as if with a life of its own...) You're next to him Charles, check it out. Is that guy wearing a live bat? (Charles goes closer to check...)

Dracula - Go ahead, touch it. (Charles does and the membranous section quivers slightly in his hand. He recoils his hand reflexively.)

Charles - It's real. (says with emotion)

Dracula - Elastic and light for flight, like a bat's wing...

Fred - Hey that's great man! He's one of the real living undead!? (The others in the room who haven't been paying attention direct their focus at Vlad.)

Charles - You can find out the rest for yourselves! (He moves away to hide behind the couch.)

Kevin - He might be rabid, I've heard about bats with it! (Vlad shrugs)

Sid – Don't be a paranoid rabbit Kevin, that's Pansy's job, ha.

Fred - No don't you guys get it? He's not a really bat. He's more like a real... vampire? (He looks at Vlad and the room is quiet, all eyes on Vlad.)

Guy - Yeah, he told us that too. (He jabs Panda in the side and she nods.)

Dracula - I don't make a habit of telling people, especially before dining, but this movie is very important. As of this moment I'm the only vampire against an army of futuristic robots. I need allies I can depend on, not store bought extras off the producer's discount rack of course.

Fred - Sure, we hear you. Though most of us don't know the first thing about how to listen... He stares at a few still talking until the room quiets down.

Panda - Have a seat (offering him a stool closer to the group that are mostly reclined on couches or the carpeted floor), but maybe you should tell us about being a vampire first. If you want to that is.

Dracula - Of course I don't expect that you follow blindly as if I were some beloved Jesus figure, there's nothing like that in the movie. Perhaps just in real life! (he laughs) But maybe someone here is devoutly religious? (About half the room, six raise their hands then most lower them leaving only Panda and Pansy with arms up. Panda smiles while Pansy looks upset again and glares at the guys who lowered their hands.)

Sid - What are you going to do to 'em man? (He tries to start a chant...) Kill the worthless Christians! (Pansy tells him to shut up and punches him hard.) The dang Christians, someone's gotta do something! Vlad?

Dracula - I'm sorry, I couldn't help myself, there isn't much to tell about myself personally. The stories you've already heard or seen are mostly true...

Guy - I know, let's take turns asking him things so we'll know the right way to act at the set!

Panda - Very practical. Let's just let him tell us stuff... like where he gets his power from? (Dracula looks to the group for volunteers...)

Charles – (summoning his nerve) Do you get power from your cape, you know like Jesus. (to the others) Remember in that movie 'The Robe' after they killed Jesus the cape kept on... you know like the pink bunny in the battery commercial. (Some nod in agreement, Pansy squints and looks annoyed.)

Dracula - His supporters would urgently insist that his body kept on as well... what is called the resurrection miracle.

Charles - I forgot. (laughs then looks serious)   Well that movie's pretty old, you'd have to be over fifty or a movie buff to even know it existed... But what I want to know really is... I know, just wait a minute... Yeah like what about Judgment Day... If you're a vampire is there an afterlife?

Dracula - Good question. If you think I'm living right now, then there certainly is. And you may want to consider that if Jesus had been a vampire before death,   if that would account for his miraculous rebirth. (stunned silence) It wouldn't be the first bit of history stolen from the vampire to be used by the church.   But don't concern yourselves, this is not so much an anti-religion movie, as a pro-vampire one!

Fred - Hey man, like have you ever had church guys after you with stakes and hammers and stuff? Or how 'bout this... suppose you didn't make it back to your coffin one day. Say you were delayed at some all night drug fest like tonight and then you got trapped in a room with mirrors all around like we have in the bathroom. Hey and then someone put a black light in there; do we have any spares? Anyway what if the tub is filled with holy water right? And garlic flavored bubble bath and there's a cross painted on the door with lamb's blood like they used for Passover! And you had to get out of there right away see? So you open the window and the sunlight streams in like a blast furnace... (His voice pitches with emotion. Dracula scowls and starts noticeably hissing. Others laugh.)

Sid - Ease up, you're starting to freak him out!

Fred - Well you get the point man.

Panda - What do you want him to do, commit suicide?

Fred - No... well I guess I was just wondering. Yeah, I mean if there was a wooden stake in the room too... Would you do yourself in man? (Dracula glares at him.) Sorry man, I guess I got carried away... It's kinda funny though, you add up all the little trivial things that might bother a person or a vampire in this case and then something as silly as garlic bath water might send him over the edge! Here Vlad, have a bowl... (Fred passes a pipe of pot.) It'll help you stay mellow... 'takes a little while though, you know the Mexican herb.

(Dracula takes the entire bowl in one inhalation...)

Fred - Tremendous!

Pansy - I heard vampires don't have reflections in mirrors because they have no souls, what about that?

Vlad - Nonsense really, not all the stories are true. I've never seen it... a soul, and I've died and been killed often in the usual sense. Whether I have one is of little consequence, a whimsy in the minds of zealots, really. And nothing to do with what a mirror might reflect.

Fred - It does if you want to play any happening Jazz, man!

Vlad - On the other hand, if I go too long without blood my form can appear to lose substance, and even more so in a mirror's reflection. (He starts to fade slightly to demonstrate... There are gasps and coughs from the group.)

Simone - You're becoming translucent.

Dracula - You can imagine that a shadow itself would have no mirror image. Fading is merely an indication that I should dine or undergo prolonged rest. Most importantly of course, dining will prevent the loss of a vampire's powers. I have never lost my powers, not in... all these years.

The Reemergence of Vlad!

Tim (Punk #7) - Yea, well how old are you man? Hell we won't remember later anyway, you may as well spill it. (Tim lights up a joint.)

Vlad - Suffice it to say I'm as old as any book you'd know and anyone from history you'd care to mention. Is that old enough?

Tim - Sounds like your age varies quite a bit, I bet they had some killer weed back then... probably worshiped it in churches and stuff, right? (laughs)

Dave - Why don't we do a documentary on dope then, hey pass it my man! (Vlad shakes his head in dismay.)

Vlad - Go ahead, quiz me. If it helps assuage your curiosities... I've known famous notables from many other times. Emperors, Queens, Warriors, Rogues and Thieves with names you might know... (As Vlad talks the smoke in the room appears to be playing tricks with his audience, twirling and swirling around their heads.)

Sid – Well how would a vampire, such as yourself, meet others of your kind and were *they* also these giants of history? (looking interested)

Vlad – Say you meet an opponent on the field of battle that doesn't die... one of the worst ways to meet a vampire I might add! Or spy something in the air at night usually before dawn flying quickly home. Mausoleums naturally are popular, very historic and help to remind us of the past. Many of the friends I've had are still in existence, as becoming a vampire is not an uncommon occurrence among my acquaintances. If all goes well with the movie you may meet some of them before long, and yes, they are of historic note.

Fred - Have you met anyone from this time period, you know drop dead industry contacts... maybe a Spielberg or Scorsese?

Vlad - Yes, both last week and also dined with his daughter by chance...

Spielberg.

Guy - Of course! He's in the movies, what d'ya think?

Fred - Well if you can get us something on the inside, serving pastries or some real bit parts then maybe I'll think about being a vampire.

Vlad - I've already left the information with our friend, Guy here. However I don't think you'll need to ask him...

Fred - Is it Megalithic Studios? (Dracula nods.) I don't know how I knew that! (He stares open eyed around the room.)

Charles – Okay the way I see it, vampires are not supposed to be like *humans*, but maybe like different species with different good points and bad points from humans. On the plus side we've got these powers, extra abilities or whatever and longevity, but then on the negative... (he ducks back down behind the couch)

Sid - On the negative, afraid of the mandatory west coast tan, religious symbols and Italian cooking herbs!

Kevin - Let's hear it for herbs! (laughs)

Guy - Yeah but all those movie people are afraid of a tan... Well except George Hamilton.

Pansy - There may be others... some.

Simone – The only negatives I see are your typical eccentric personality traits, except the deal about the wooden stakes and what human wouldn't be afraid of that? If anything that might do more to prove your human. It means you've just got a heart that pumps blood and located in the chest. Maybe if it was on the other side or pumped green stuff like the vulcans in Star Trek? Then I'd be freaked.

The Reemergence of Vlad!

Guy – Yeah, well I'd become a vampire and a vulcan if it meant I'd meet T'Pol from the Star Trek Enterprise or that sweet Borg, 7 of 9, green blood and all! (Panda smacks him.)

Kevin – Guy's definitely not human. Man that's just not right... especially when everyone's an alien in the New Generation show. It's just not the same.

Pansy – Hey it's like how the mention of girls can make (she looks around the room) Sid feel like an alien, am I right? (She waits for his response but he is feigning sleep.) Hey what were we talking about? Oh yeah... Vulcans.

Guy – No, vampires. Don't worry Vlad we'll be in your movie if we survive the party tonight... (he sighs and swallows some beer.)

Pansy - Right. I think what it is about the Dracula legend is like this morbid preoccupation with death, you know for people who want to spend time worrying about their final days. Like that Nixon book? It may be popular sure but most people aren't that interested. Look according to legend the Dracula monster sleeps in a crypt or coffin, right? He's also got no blood, no complexion, and goes around wearing formal clothes all the time but only at night so people won't see how bad he looks. (The others look at Vlad worriedly.) It all points to the fact that this Dracula guy is dead or just about as near it as you can get! The *undead* rap is just a cover, huh? Oh, sorry Vlad...

Vlad - Yes, (looking amused) well blood is the most important thing of course, that a vampire needs. Some have compared their effect on society to that of doctors. They endanger the lives of patients with major surgeries and powerful drugs, and then extract large fees. So too the vampire takes a toll on the lives of mortals to an extent, lives may be lost but for some... existence is prolonged. It is the way of nature! The stronger extract sustenance from the weaker.

Pansy - That may be but there's always been a lot of mythology about death hasn't there? Vampires naturally fill that niche nicely I'd say. Simple biology, therefore they must be real... (Fred mutters, 'I'd like to fill her niche.' Sid rousing gives him the thumbs up.) What I don't see is the reason for the vampires' problem with mirrors. Does it show their true age and the fact they're not among the living? (Vlad stares at her with piercing eyes, obviously growing mildly disturbed. The others do what they can to distract him. Guy massages him.)

Fred - Not the mirrors again...

Guy - Vlad, that must be short for Vladamir, right? Vladamir, get it? Vlad a mirror! (laughs at his joke)

Fred - Listen sister it's not that they don't like what they see, just *sometimes* they can't see themselves. You heard him.

Charles - Wait, you know I bet back in olden times there probably weren't many mirrors. Who even knows when they got invented? People probably just had to use a bowl of water instead. A mirror-like reflection but not a mirror because if you touch it the image disappears!

Fred - What's the point, man?

Charles – Well maybe a mirror is just a symbol for water. 'Probably water's the thing they don't like. After all they sleep on dirt so they probably don't have great hygiene. They may even be more like cats, who hate water, than bats...

Fred - No only witches don't like water, everyone knows that!

Charles - The mirror could be a symbol of purity then. Clouded water

106

wouldn't show a reflection, so not seeing yourself in it could be a bad sign. You'd get diseases or parasites... cholera which kills millions right, from bad water can turn you into a vampire! Or if cleanliness is next to Godliness the only thing left for vampires is uncleanliness.

Fred – So they're just afraid to see themselves because they're pure evil... makes sense I guess.

Charles - You're forgetting they're not afraid of water or reflections, they simply...

Several at once - Don't have one! (they laugh and look at Dracula who looks unaffected even distracted.)

Dracula – Think of it like this, does a shadow cast a reflection? It cannot.

Pansy – Now I'm bored, thanks Charles. Why don't you just save it for your next term paper on feline history. I have a cat and my cat is always very clean regardless of how much she hates water!

Sid - I'm getting restless, all this talk about licking! (laughs)

Pansy - You jerk.

Panda - Who cares already, Pansy's right. This is getting disgusting and boring. Vlad knows you're just trying to humor him. (She looks over at Vlad.) So if he doesn't feel like proving anything now (smiles at Vlad), I say we do something. Maybe go someplace, it's still early.

Kevin - Want to fire up another bone first? Anybody? (Vlad is about to speak when interrupted...)

Fred - No man, we're going out, remember?

Sid – Wait I've got to be high if I'm going out with you guys. You're not even of the female persuasion!

Fred – Cripes will you shut up ah your mouth?

Guy - How 'bout a brownie instead. There's a tray in the fridge!

Fred - Sure let's go to some vampire hangout with the man himself, like the old movie set for a Batman sequel or one of those kinky clubs off the boulevard. Kids get off there drinking real blood and stuff. I've seen 'em, dudes with their dates biting each other or even using knives right there in public. It's insane! Most of them have got stuff pierced for vamp jewelry, and stuff that probably shouldn't be.

Pansy - I don't know, 'sounds like a crime scene. I don't think I want to be busted when I'm high.

Sid - Yeah that's what you always say.

Fred – It'll be great!

Guy – And we've got the main dude himself to protect us... So what if it's raided, what are they going to do... breath-alizers for brownies?

Simone - (mouth full of brownie) They'll maul us with their dogs! I saw it on Top Cops once...

Casey - I might be paranoid... but what if (whispering) you know, what if our dude is from the vampire club and he's like their leader or something see, and he's on a mission to convert more of them... us to vampires with life-time memberships!

Vlad - We will go to the club of you're choosing, though a cult of vampire worshipers sounds irresistibly appealing I must admit.

Guy - Forget it! (to Casey) He's never heard of those places. He told us before, Vlad's just arrived in Hollywood for the first time recently to do his movie! He hasn't been anywhere yet. The vampire scene it is!

The Reemergence of Vlad!

1

They start to leave, Dracula reluctantly shrugs his shoulders then helps Pansy with her jacket. Others head for a quick mouthwash or grab a brownie for the road trying to juggle putting on jackets, leaving the apartment and eating at the same time. None is in a condition to drive but they are fortunate to hop a bus that brings them a short distance to the commercial district where they can walk down side streets for the remaining blocks.

Simone - (They depart the bus.) Since no one's heard my spin on this mythical beast, the vampire, yet... No offense Vlad. I'd like to confess that I once thought about it though... what if you know. (Some of the punks look at him sideways.) Really sometimes I think about stuff, even when I'm not stoned. (They laugh.)

Panda - We know, ever since one of your teachers had the bad judgment to say you had potential. She wrongly sent you to some specially degreed guidance counselor a year early when she really wanted you deported to Mexico.

Simone - I'm serious, when we're vampires like Vlad we can fly to Mexico, just the two of us... and Vlad. (He puts his arm around Panda, she taps it off.) And of course Guy can come with. (Guy frowns)

Fred - Don't forget to bring some grass on the way back, man. (A street sign placed strangely near the middle of the side walk almost clips him.) Whoa Bundy! (Dracula smiles.)

Simone – Anyway I think vampire lore stems from nobility, the royals in the past, maybe the Dark Ages. Think of it, back then if a royal personage got himself in trouble they'd just make up some legend to explain things, the darker or scarier the better! And then of course banish any witnesses to the dungeon or the castle tower. A lot of modern parallels probably exist with Hollywood celebrities except the banishment part. Just look at the stuff celebrities do... it's all in the tabloids. Living in Hollywood it's easy to tell most of that stuff's true, but they rarely admit anything and sometimes sue over it or try to vanish like a vampire. Poof! (They gage Vlad's reaction.) Of course some get tagged doing something but the worse that happens is they end up with a new wife or girlfriend. Of course having a huge divorce action is probably like having a stake driven through... But they never get thrown in jail and the main thing they all want is irresistibility and longevity, just like vampires. Besides, they don't eat real food, they're in great shape, they're always going for that erotic moonlight kiss... drunk from all their affairs... their conquests like blood to a vampire! And even with their hi-tech extremely private lives, they still get caught by paparazzi because they're at it so often. (He laughs.)

Fred – Don't forget drugs man. That's what they're into. That's why they have all those plush detox centers near LA...

Guy - Sounds romantic, eh Vlad? When we're stars all we have to care about is being in love and a good supplier. Hey that sounds like me and my

The Reemergence of Vlad!

Panda Bear!

Panda – A lot of celebs seem to be gay as well, right Guy?

Guy – Well for sure but you keep tabs on those so I don't have to. (He gives her a wink.) And stars all have to have personal trainers, that's how they stay in such great shape. Naturally there's no trouble keeping thin cause they're too busy zoning out on herb, which they don't worry about because they've got great security. Once Vlad is a big-name I'll bet he'll be planning some hellacious parties at his mansion. (whispering to Panda) Hey stay close to him once we get inside... don't let any weirdos get too chummy. He's ours!

Panda - You are gay, I don't believe it! Vlad help! (She leans closer to Vlad.)

Guy - Shhh! You dummy. Vlad'll hear you. Here I'll bite you and save him the trouble! (He lunges at her, pretending to go for her jugular. The group stops though and restrains him since they've arrived at the entrance to the club. A large set of fangs is painted above the entrance, and the sidewalk in front of the door is red.)

2

With Dracula at the lead they enter the nightclub. Immediately a young girl in a provocative outfit comes up to them. The music's loud. She takes Dracula to a back room where it's quieter and roomy. His friends (the punks) join him and they sit. The girl is on his lap. She asks him...

Vampire Girl - If you were to spell the word 'love' backwards, how would it sound?

Dracula - (utters) Evol... Evil?

Vampire Girl - Right! (She removes the black shawl covering her upper right breast revealing a tattoo of the word, evil. The left breast reads, love. She laughs and kisses Vlad hard on the neck, then leaves him.)

Guy - Vlad's a natural in a place like this. She's telling her friends about you, you could probably get a hundred extras if you want... you wouldn't need to shell out anything for wardrobes. (As he talks several club regulars file in to the room. They all wear black, appear gaunt and have red contact lenses. They look at Vlad with interest and sit at the periphery of the group.)

Vlad - I may need an army of vampires. I'll forgo my salary if necessary. (His voice can be easily heard above the pulsing music.)

Guy - So Vlad, why don't you tell us how this vampire business started anyway. Before you mentioned Jesus might be one. Have they been around that long, even Dracula didn't make a name for himself until what, the fifteenth century A.D.? According to Transylvania tour books...

Vlad - That may be true but vampires have existed long before that, since the dawn of Roman times and beyond... And their influence has been felt in subtle ways. You probably never realized that Jesus, for instance, actually preached sermons of death when he praised the afterlife... for what fanatic's corpse has ever benefited? They may have been respected in life but in death, only deluded... Only severely affected fanatics claiming to be reborn and thereby experiencing an afterlife of sorts before death have reaped any fruits of religious faith. That is the extent of their claim to have conquered death. The vampire on the other hand is merely concerned with living, having left the realm of dying to mortal humans. Though vampires can only extol the values of being undead as you know, this far outweighs the alternatives. And until this new cyborg menace I didn't think any existed...

Vampires (from the club) - (mostly girls shout in unison) Master!

Fred - What can vampires contribute to society though if they're only alive at night?

A Club Member - The same thing you do!

Vlad - There is no reason to think society has to proceed to chaos just because humans have become vampires... I admit I don't picture myself actively working to improve society, as some politician, but then I do have a fairly good excuse... being among the first and naturally one of the leading vampires. But there hasn't been much occasion until now... to do much leading. I've already accumulated a comfortable level of wealth... And it is precisely to this end wherein lies the allure and ultimate promise of life as a vampire. Given enough time all should obtain their desired ambition or wealth. And none should have to make much more than the standard sacrifice in lifestyle or deathstyle rather toward this end!

Panda - (looking at the mesmerized club vampire girls with disdain) Why hate religion so much though? Churches do a lot of good.

Vlad - They sometimes do perhaps, but only a fraction of their resource will go to this. The majority is spent on their buildings and finery, bright colors and extravagant garments. And of course salaries for themselves, the deserving priests, padres and preachers. They deny it but they create a class of false privilege, in order to perceive themselves as better in the eyes of their neighbors or other zealots. (Panda shrugs.) With this movie my concern is with science however and the new technology more than religion... What these producers are predicting may soon come to be, whether they realize their accuracy or not. I've been following the developments in cybernetic research myself, at least. I'm alerted to it, and will use my influence to alert the viewing public. For we will not be just the ones to suffer if what they predict comes to be. What would stop immortalized robots from creating larger and stronger models of themselves eliminating both humans and vampires in the process? After that a world of machines would kill itself from boredom and sterility.

Guy - A definite problem, but don't worry we're here to help.

Kevin - (under his breath) Vampires are sterile too, what's the big deal? (louder) Hey Countess, I need a refill! (The club vampires give him the evil eye, then one leaves, returning in a little while with a tray of red drinks.)

Vampire Girl - The master's thirsty! (She laughs and tries to serve Dracula. He refuses. The others take drinks.)

Vlad - (to the waitress) Perhaps I'll soon be having what you're having... (He smiles exposing some of his prodigious canines.) Why don't we ask the club vampires why they choose to be what they are?

Club Member - (shakes his head proudly exposing small bones piercing his ears and a tattoo on his neck of Angelina Jolie's lips...) Sure, why not. I like your frock Count Vlad. I have to say I've seen pictures of your namesake, the Impaler himself and the resemblance is striking... Anyway we here at the club are all vampires in some way, because we all want the same thing, to feel as young as we want to be and to do whatever we want... knowing we can because we're all immortal vampires. Some of us may be older or younger but we don't worry about growing old, neurotic or feeble, because we don't... If you're the master we'll do what you ask and please take your pick of anyone here to feed on.

Vampire Girls - (in unison) Take us! Take us! (They gaze longingly.)

Another Club Member - One thing I'd like to know if we may benefit from your endless experience... is how much blood is enough? A lot of us drink the real stuff and well is there anything like a minimum or maximum, say? Or I guess you know when you've had enough?

Dracula - It is true, too many treat the matter lightly relying on whim, mood or often how the blood tastes at the time. (The club vampires react with surprise and excitement.) Vampires with little concern about it can be gluttonous and leave a litany of corpses in their wake. I for one believe the true nature of the vampire is one of subtle seduction, leaving the victim just enough blood for life but wanting to give more. And that's the essence of a proper conversion of course... repeated on successive nights until the victim, ah *person* used to existing on the edge or fringes between worlds of light and dark must make a choice... death or the immortal life of a vampire. As you might expect the success rate is high...

Panda - Some choice! (Dracula's eyes grow subtly red.)

Dracula - Naturally a vampire would prefer to have many victims to just one at a time, all trying to continue with the remnants of their former lives and providing a ready source of blood. Once a vampire is formed, released from the human bond, the blood is no longer sustaining to other vampires unless that vampire has himself just dined. It is the curious condition of immortal blood that it has only the power to create but not sustain a vampire. Though I've met some who would disagree, they are definitely wrong and discover their error eventually, usually when it is too late. (The club members and his new friends regard him with a mixture of rapt curiosity and horror.) Of course a vampire can maintain a certain appearance no matter what his feeding habits. A powerful one can will himself to appear larger, stronger, fearsome or even as an animal but will always revert when relaxed and in his coffin. Since altering appearances requires more effort, a prolonged period of relaxation will follow, sometimes several days...

Guy - Hey man, you gotta believe him, don't you? He's been there. Look, even the club members are totally awed... (The vampire girls are staring at Vlad, red liquid from their drinks drooling from their mouths.) I say let's go for it. Yeah let's let him do us all right now, and be vampires! (The others nod agreement though some are a little hesitant at first, including Panda. The club members' eyes widen with anticipation.) What d'ya say, Count? Can you drink your limit tonight?

Dracula - (Eying them with surprise...) Why yes, I suppose. In the old days I would occasionally *do* as you say an entire village, small villages, in order to help prevent dissension and discovery. I couldn't live up to my reputation as Dracula, of the first, oldest and most terrifying vampires if I didn't rampage from time to time.

Guy - We can still be in the movie right? After...

Dracula - All of you! (raising his arms wide) Come to me children and receive my gift...

3

As Dracula speaks a fine mist wafts through the club. People in the other room who were about to leave stop and return to seats. Couples who were talking animatedly become calm, and even the band begin a more relaxed dazed style of play. In the back room with Dracula, the vampire girls are first to jump up offering their necks. Guy takes hold of Panda's arm and maneuvers her closer to Vlad and in front of himself while smiling. Dracula drinks in a quick and perfunctory manner, almost businesslike as he goes from one to the next. One girl from the group offers a condom package as he approaches but only succeeds in lodging it in his mouth before she is overcome by his presence.

Tim - (waiting his turn and talking with a vampire club member) Hey this is kind of like holy communion only more realistic, isn't it? But wine is supposed to represent actual blood anyway. If I were religious this might be like the Pope serving communion, the major difference being that Dracula, in our case is only receiving the sacrament, not dispensing. (He laughs.)

Club Member – Yes, only after a lengthy initiation are young vampires allowed to drink from the font of life. (appears mesmerized)

Casey - (waiting near the back of the throng) Do you think he'll tell us when we'll know we're... you know, turned? How are we supposed to know this stuff? (Dracula approaches and bites them without a word. While biting the group individually in the back room a club member goes to the main room. He finds the lead singer of 'Eat My Gore' on break trying to recover from too many beers. The musician perks up his ears and grabs the microphone after hearing out the urgently whispered message.)

Lead Singer - (loudly) Friends and Vampires and Disciples of Death! I've just gotten word that Club Dracula has been visited by its namesake! That's right, the otherworldly master of vampires himself, Dracula! (awed sighs and cheers) The Lord of Death and Darkness offers us a communion of blood, for those who seek his immortal gift! (cheers, some pass out... One girl, a newcomer, voices a concern... 'What about AIDS?')

Dracula - (appearing suddenly in their midst) In my blood there can be no other life but mine own. In your blood will be ah new life... with the dark gift, your first visit of immortality. (He envelopes her with leathery soft black wings and drinks.)

New Club Member – (to his friend) Hey this isn't anything too heavy... like the trip that guy Jim Jones laid on his people, do you think?

Regular Member – (the friend) Naw man, take it easy. The guy's for real, check the wings. I think he's the main dude, not some goth stand-in or band effects stunt. I bet he's the head guy, you know (pointing downward) from down there, the underworld!

New Member - I say let's ask him.

Regular Member - Naw, we better not, what if he gets mad? You don't want to miss your chance to become a real vampire?

New Member - Yeah I guess so...

4

As Dracula moves among the snaking line formed by the orderly crowd he bites each one lightly on the neck extracting small amounts of blood, in a near painless mesmerizing ritual...

Girl on line - (talking to her friend as they ready for Dracula's approach and notice blood dripping from his fangs) They say if you look at his eyes first it won't hurt... (Just then another girl let's out a small cry of pain. Dracula excuses himself for a moment, finds a sturdy wooden table and proceeds to punch out neat holes with teeth and jaws.)

5

With freshly sharpened teeth he continues with the two girls next in line. They feel no pain but are dazed and weakened. As he reaches the last of the crowd Dracula's eyes glow a steady red-orange, then grow brighter and appear golden while his physical shape also grows, changing to an even more powerful dark winged creature. He spreads the leather webbing of his awesome wings about the room unfolding and releasing hidden layers and talons until they encircle almost the entire inner recesses of the club and its patrons. For a moment everything is deathly silent and as if everyone is listening to his or her own personal message of urgent hope, desire and need. Necks crane and heads bow in order to better perceive Dracula's silent prayer to them. 'I am with you now and you will feel my power as surely as the sun... In your blood lighting a path to sensation and feelings, touching the smallest nerves, opening the weakest vessels is my blood... The dark blood, my gift to you and just once more and you too may hold the key to everlasting death and whatever else you may choose. You will soon seek the earth by day, returning to it to rest each night... until you will feel the thirst, your immortal thirst and know... Until then return to me here each night... Please also join me if you will in making a new movie; you'll have little need of direction by the time we start filming... which should please the directors!

A huge rumbling of laughter erupts from deep within of Dracula's strange form. He begins to dissipate, slowly fading, blending with the thin mist, leaving shadows and textures where his monstrous wings and body had been until finally there only remains a cloud of amorphous matter seeping through windows, doors and ceiling vents... Someone nearing the club entrance on the street rushes in to inform them he's just seen a large cat-like animal, very black and quietly walking along the sidewalk. It might be a panther though he couldn't be sure since he's never been to a zoo and doesn't care for nature shows on T.V. It definitely wasn't anything normal... No one in the club is too surprised. The band checks its new pierced neck look in the mirror and like it.

6

Next evening Dracula puts in a brief appearance at the movie set where preparations are underway to begin shooting the first scenes in a couple days. He finds a director and tells him about problems with the writers and reasserts his claim of artistic license, contract rights, etc. The director, afterward leaves memos for others on staff and crew to humor Dracula saying... 'He thinks he's a star! You know the type...' Dracula then finds the script department where a lone script consultant is at work. He attempts to hypnotize her, staring and baring his canines, but only gives her a bad scare. She reports him to an assistant producer who consoles her saying, 'Happens all the time with big ego stars. Don't worry we have memos out on him. He'll say the material works better his way, but what he really wants is more exposure, or a nomination, or he could be after my job. Anyway just ignore him. We're not here to win awards, only money! Remember that. (She walks away frustrated.)

Dracula then returns to the nightclub. Only about half the previous night's patrons are in attendance. He notices that many of his bite marks are misplaced or sloppy. Some have marks down near their chests, others under the chins. He blames it on the fact young people tend to move about a lot and recalls how some thought he wanted to dance, not bothering to pay attention. At least most of Guy's group has returned. They want to know more about the movie. He bites them eagerly.

Dracula - Much has been written about recent advances with cyborg technology, and a lot of it very distressing. I've just come from the movie set and unfortunately they are not the least bit interested. We'll just have to take liberties on the set... Can you imagine a life more bereft of soul than that as a computerized cyborg creature? They may contain human memories but after activation they'd remember everything in the same fashion as any boring computer... That's what you'd assume, wouldn't you? (Though dazed they seem to agree.) Not so, I've read they can selectively quantify the way an individual, person thinks i.e. preferences, priorities, dislikes, even biological mood swings due to both typical and unusual patterns of behavior... such as if the person is health conscious, stressed, alcoholic, caffeine addicted or other, even sleeping patterns.

Guy - What's your beef then?

Dracula - The apparent perfection makes the threat all the more insidious. In time converted cyborgs would *change* from the human habits of previous life adapting to the reality of a computer hardware existence removing the reminders of past human frailties. Increased analytical and memory capacity would be available but would need limits or a hostile takeover of society might result, to say the least.

Guy – You're saying the cyborgs would become so smart that they'd want to cause a hostile takeover and *kill all humans...* Hey just like *Futurama* predicted! Police would have to revise their policies I bet.

Charles - But identity and existence should be enhanced overall, allowing them to take on roles they might never have imagined as humans... much as ourselves as vampires. And with increased mental capabilities, there might be a true Utopia or euphoric existence.

Guy – Yeah but only if they *kill all humans* remember, and the vampires too no doubt! And the reason Vlad here has decided to rise out of the pumpkin patch, eh Vlad?

Dracula – (taking the cue to wax poetic for his cause once more) I think the key word is *existence*. Life as a computer might be just that, mere existence. Real feelings of urgent need, desire and sensation would be artificial... wouldn't they? Vampire blood may be cold, and most physical functions undetectable but the function of bone and blood is for the most part a crucial requisite for life, even as an undead. It could never be otherwise. (He excuses himself and makes the rounds of other club members, biting with abandon... making their conversions complete.)

7

The next night group members meet again at the club and converse... 'Hey do you think we're vampires yet?' 'No, didn't you listen, he said you'd know when it happens... the thirst!' 'Well my mom didn't recognize me when I came in last night. Maybe because I hid in the cellar crawlspace all day!'

Vlad - (Arrives to see most of his converts are still with him.) Favored children, you may want to know more about me as you face your vampire future...

Guy - And movie careers! When are we going to be actors? (they laugh)

Vlad - As you know vampires have been in existence for millennia... I assumed the name Dracula... an extraction from my title, Prince Vlad, son of Dracul at a time when the vampire tradition had reached a pinnacle of refinement and popularity. In life I relished the dual character of merciless savagery in battle while placing love for my young bride on the highest alter. I lost her to sacrificial suicide, and upon seeing the endless flow of blood as it marked the steps of our altar I made a vow that stays in my deepest heart. Soon after, as the legend goes, I was bestowed the gift of the vampire and continue to this day or so they say as a symbol or testament to the culmination, the quintessence of vampirism and immortal life...

Guy – Legend... Or so they say? So you didn't really become a vampire then?

Vlad - Actually I first died centuries before, but as I've said the tradition grew strongest at that time... (some shake their heads) You see history is seldom what it seems. And while I may not be the first vampire to walk the earth, I've attained a certain status or notable notoriety and deservedly so. I'm therefore justified taking the role as spokesman for vampires and our ultimate cause.

Guy - Is there anything else about vampire history we should know?

Vlad - Occasionally I've sought past truths from older and other less formidable vampires. You are no doubt aware of our close ties to early religions... There were fanatical attempts to explain away the mystic somewhat less refined powers of the oldest vampires. An often pathetic comedy really, that some people so repulsed at the idea of immortal life of vampires became hysterical zealots for causes imaginary and in mimicry of us. The problem exists to this day! But I like to think it was worse in the earlier times.

Guy - Why if vampires are the true unseen powers of this world... haven't they had more impact?

Vlad - The early ones have never possessed much desire, though I say it is more to do with character, to influence groups larger than the smallest villages or communities. For a vampire to be found within the confines of a city was rare... a boarding house or small condominium maybe nowadays. Nonetheless they did have influence, just through existing... but it can be almost embarrassing really, the constant lack of character. For the most part they were never missed during the day, and absence at important times simply reinforced their lack of vitality and resolve. They could wield powers of hypnotic persuasion but somehow never collectively or to best advantage. To hear them there is always a blame... the threat of recognition, exposed vulnerabilities, lack of access to the opportunities of the day. But many excuses relate to selfish fear and imagined disability. And down the centuries I've often avoided contact with other vampires, growing tired of their reasons for apathy... until I've become no better than they. But I've decided to change and even now try acting. I can't say as I'm completely pleased with how my first film went, the directors were bent on projecting the same ridiculous cliches for the most part...

Sid – Hey don't beat yourself up, I saw it and it wasn't half bad. (mild cheering from those that had seen it)

Fred – Yeah, you rock Vlad! (more cheers) Rock on!

Vlad - By the way let me take a minute to thank most of you who have already registered as extras to be in my next picture. I feel humans deserve a chance or at least a choice between immortal life of real feelings, and existence with only a mechanized virtual reality. We can give them that chance through our performance on the big screen! (cheering)

Guy - I guess we'll have to take your word for that Vlad. (Dracula frowns. Guy looks to the others...) We can take his word for that, right? (subdued cheers)

Vlad - Thank you. Well to rehearse your roles, and now that you've had time to reflect, are there any new ideas of what a vampire is for the other's benefit? Maybe after going home and asking your parents? Hopefully something more than scavengers at the edges of cities... living on what society has tossed aside: the homeless vagrants, wayward prostitutes and drug dealers...

Simone - What I've heard is that vampire 'myth' began with groups of incurable insomniacs and carousers... maybe like us, content to coexist, just blend in at first. (some laughter) Scholars differ (more laughter) but most seem to agree... they would use any excuse including the most morbid and macabre imaginable for their nightly escapades in order to not arouse undo local reaction. The fact is these incessant partiers collapsed from exhaustion at dawn in places of seclusion such as mausoleums or cemeteries, wanting to avoid the disruption of families to which they belonged and which couldn't understand, and who said they'd been cursed or worse. Anyway if discovered during the day they appeared so hideous, lying amongst the crypts or freshly dug graves they were rationalized to be suffering a horrible affliction... that of a vampire. And at first they were to be pitied and there were frantic efforts to redeem their souls and recover their health. But most vampires, having once succumbed to nightly drinking and lewd encounters, stalking and other unacceptable pursuits soon lost all pretense of a normal life, and became social pariahs to roam at night feeding on the good intentions and the very life's blood of others... who too in time often became corrupted under the cunning influence of these despicable creatures! They could be compared to rock musicians and entertainers of modern times. (They laugh.)

Vlad - Well except for that part about hideous appearance, you're right concerning their habits... especially the young vampires! Isn't there something else that might set them apart from other humans though?

Guy - Thinness. Vampires are very thin, gaunt. That can be a frightening appearance, almost hideous! Some would say it's repulsive, someone like my girlfriend Panda who's a little overweight! (They laugh.) Yeah only stars or super models actually look good being that thin. All I think of when I see them is how incredibly vain they must be... looking so much better than everyone and loving every minute! Hey, but some blood is high in cholesterol. Wouldn't a vampire put on weight if he's not careful?

Vlad - There are preferences for blood just as there are with wine.

Guy - Right, all this talk about blood is making me a little thirsty! It's a little salty isn't it? I mean (trying to change the subject) you've probably been involved in some nasty wars. Have you done much fighting since your 'Impaler' days?

Vlad - No, I try to avoid the confusion of countries when they are in the throes of battle... though sometimes it was not always immediately apparent, being often alienated from the populace... Well there have been forgettable occurrences. I was once under the Russian front. They were suddenly fighting over the location I'd chosen as a shallow grave for the day's rest. I was unearthed by tank fire but due to the heavy smoke of battle found time for reconcealment under the ruptured ground.

Tim - Do you suppose you ever met Hitler? Now there's a sick dude. Was he a vampire? He had all the blood he could handle.

Vlad - Actually I barely knew of him. I wasn't as concerned as others with the current events of the time as perhaps I should have been in retrospect. He couldn't have been a vampire and hold a high profile public office... completely against our nature. Of course he was influential, a typical vampire trait. To keep his grip on society, his lust for power probably drove him to war. Then he was proven very ineffectual and deficient, a possible indication of vampirism at the last.

Dave - Well vampires don't have to be too bright do they?

Vlad - And a vampire wouldn't need to control armies of mortals just to ensure a constant or ready supply of blood.

Tim - Maybe the war was a ruse, you know... Protection for some kind of army of vampires. The SS?

Fred - That's pretty far-fetched man.

Guy - Well look how many drinks our Count here has had the past few nights... A small army of vampires might be able to put an entire country to some use... blood farming?

Dave - Hey and you know they say Hitler was weird and eccentric, kind of like the exotic quirks vampires have... because they're all serial murderers!

Dracula - Really, my motives are sincere. I want to help mortals. Have I killed anyone yet?

Tim - (whispering with the other) Kind of sounds like you have before though, doesn't it?

Dave - Maybe lots of times! (The group doesn't look at him, thinking how sordid his past might be...)

Dracula - I really must admire that Jesus character at times like these. I'm sure he never went through anything like this. Though I've bitten fifty or more of you several times, and on the most vital, life-sensitive areas...

Pansy - He's talking about our necks right?

Dracula - A few degrees more force, a tad more hunger and well... mistakes can be deadly.

Pansy - What does he mean, deadly?

Dave - You know, death, like a rotting corpse...

Panda - Oh. Well I know this is still morning for a vampire but I'd better leave. I forgot to eat today... and it's already night! (She smiles revealing hungry looking large canines.)

Guy - Wait. I've got another question, just one more. (turns to Vlad) It's the way you're always preaching against Jesus. You wouldn't be the anti-Christ? (looking worried)

Dracula - Why is it the anti-Christ this, or Hitler that! You'll see to your chagrin that it is the name, Jesus, spoken with passion, never that of Dracula! It should be that there is an anti-Vampire or anti-Dracula, just once. Simply because God *ascends* to life everlasting while the vampire must descend into the earth for like purpose, that the other receives top ranking, the popular appeal! Ancient vampires were the first to conquer death and their stories borrowed, changed and molded into the idea of righteous afterlife by fanatic religious writers. You will learn.

Guy - Yeah well, we can see you've had it pretty rough... We better let you get some rest. (Dracula rises and waves them off.) See you on the set then! (He departs.) Dracula! (Guy calls after him.) You forgot... to drink. (He massages his neck but Dracula has gone.)

PART IV

THE COMMUNION

Dracula rushes home in search of Renfield.

Vlad - Renfield! (loudly) We must ready ourselves for the ceremony of the elders... Did you remember... Were you able to bring the supplies?

Renfield - Yes master.

Vlad - The new ones will need guidance. There are many young vampires now to help with the movie but I need insurance. The success of the movie and the cause of vampirism itself is too important to be entrusted to them alone. The old ones must be called...

Renfield - I could place telephone calls in town to see if they might be reached more quickly?

Vlad - No, I doubt it. And the impact would be lost. Besides it's been a while, they may have newer names and addresses. And the excuses! I'd prefer not to have to listen to those. They'll be summoned in the old way or not at all!

Renfield - Yes I have the items in this box.

Vlad - Good, bring it to the clearing in back.

Renfield - Where we burned the lamps and mirrors?

Vlad - (hisses) Yes. (He excavates a shallow depression in the ground.) Did you bring the fire extinguishers as well?

Renfield - (reading the side) Containing flame retardant chemicals, and a nice shade of red for decoration if it's empty!

Vlad - (Placing a heavy bowl with carvings of a dragon and a horned centaur on its sides in the pit...) Alright then Renfield, the ingredients! First, holy water. (Renfield removes a small flask from the box and makes a quick motion over it with the other hand before emptying the contents in the bowl.) Now the cross. (Again he fishes out a modest cross of wood and quickly drops it in the urn.) Now the likeness of the... Anti-Vampire. (Renfield looks confused.) The Savior... Renfield? (Renfield produces an 8 x 10 Sunday school picture of Jesus.) Very Good... And of myself... (He starts tearing and chewing at his fingertips causing the nails to splinter, and tosses some shards in the bowl. Renfield shows him a pair of nail clippers and Dracula relents, using them.) Something old, Renfield some of my coffin earth if you don't mind... (Renfield is ready with a child's bucket of dirt and scoop.) A drop of golden sun... (He scrapes his fingers along Renfield's shirt, taking some of the material, lighting it and adding to the contents. There is a brief phosphorus like flare and a green glowing flame appears.) Me a name, no, no. This is no time for merriment eh Renfield? (Renfield smiles..) A drop of liquid night then, (smiling) The dark gift itself... (Using the middle fingernails of his unclipped hand he then punctures two wounds into his wrist. Dark blood runs briefly into the receptacle. The flame shifts larger, throws sparks and a turns a bluish hue.

The Reemergence of Vlad!

The sky rumbles and the earth shakes slightly. The night darkens as the moon already high in the sky appears more prominent and takes on a deep red hue. Dracula chants...)

'Remembered now again as in oldest times
To those wherein abide darkest earth and demon wine,
I bring ye forth with wrath and vengeance mine,
And make life again 'this ancient rhyme.
With my own blood I light this hearth
So that immortal eyes may see and know the curse!
Join me now, be with the first...
To join me now, you must find the source...
Find the source, of this ancient **thirst!**

(They wait a moment but nothing happens.) That one rarely works, does it? Yet it has elegance, except that line... about 'immortal eyes' could sound like a verb. What do you think, Renfield?

Renfield - I'm not sure master.

Vlad - I'll try another. (While Dracula thinks Renfield sights something crawling on the ground and pounces. He adds the captured insect to the pot.)

Of dust and bone and ancient earth

Of ageless blood, forgotten birth

Demon's breath and dragon fire

I summon ye 'the highest pyre

*I call you now, your name, **Vampire!***

He finishes the incantation and a dark funnel cloud, tinged black and red starts thinly over them and uncoils widening and winding skyward until seeming to reach the moon itself...

Vlad - Well, now we wait. Eh Renfield? (He turns and heads back to the house.)

Renfield - Yes master. It's very exciting... I'll prepare the main hall for (the return of) the old ones... I'll try to be worthy. (He looks back at the cloud and retrieves the bowl, dumping the ashes.)

The Reemergence of Vlad!

1

The next night just after midnight Dracula is seated at a large table in the main hall reading a newspaper. The headlines read, 'Strange weather occurrence originates locally, never before documented!' There is a long canoe shaped wooden dish on the table filled with a burning liquid, a hypnotic blue flame dances. There are several knocks on the door... Renfield rushes to the door, looks out through a small window, nods to Vlad and opens the door completely, pinning himself. Imposing figures enter. One with a dark purple cape, another's is black velvet and the last wears a shroud of black leather.

Dracula - Ah Cyrule, One, Ram. How are you? Come in.

One - Yes Vlad, you're looking... well recognizable and no doubt feel as you look. (laughing) We decided to wait until the camera trucks left. Apparently others are curious about the strange weather in the area.

Dracula - Renfield spent the day shooing them away... people watching for aliens, wanting to see the house, some demanding explanations. Some things rarely change much in time do they? Come, let's toast the longest friendships on Earth!

Cyrule - (sitting down) I don't see any drinks Vlad... (Renfield remains hidden behind the door.)

Ram - What's it been a couple hundred years, I hardly recall the occasion... Oh yes how could I forget, the printing of your first book by that Stoker fellow. 'Popular sure but not much cause for celebration. Should have written it yourself like I said.

Dracula - Well I didn't have to write it, I lived it and this time it is something even more fantastic and I'll need your support. So what of the others? They're not all in London to use smog as an excuse!

One - There have been casualties Vlad, I'm sad to say, some... but then it also takes time for the smoke to circle around. Not as simple as blood through a vein. I expect Osiris may be here in a night or two, still residing in the fertile Nile valley you know.

Vlad - Yes of course.

One - Where is that demonomist servant of yours? I hope well or as well as can be expected. (Renfield slinks from behind the front door quietly to the kitchen.)

Vlad - An interesting term that, servant of evil, isn't it? Hardly appropriate... Anyway, he's the same though recently he was confronted with the prospect of a girlfriend. But Renfield's beast is under a rather stern control.

One - Still won't consummate his powers on human blood? How long has it been... five hundred years, and still afraid to admit he's a vampire?

Cyrule - A half breed without powers is all he is, an abomination. Throw him out and leave him on his own. He'll learn soon enough.

Vlad – He (Renfield) does live on his own. He sees to my needs not the reverse. He believes himself to be whatever it is he is, just not a vampire... I imagine there are reasons.

One - 'Can't bring himself to drink blood from the neck of the living... not even once?

Vlad - He's afraid of the sight of it, I suppose. Just as I shudder at the sight of what he prefers to dine on, every possible crawling thing from birds and rodents to meal worms. It's no wonder he's forfeit everything save existence itself, but to him it doesn't seem to matter much. He also doesn't require a coffin, goes about his affairs during overcast days with no ill effect and as I've said actually subsists almost entirely on insects and possibly a few birds, which fortunately for him do contain some blood as well.

Cyrule - Disgusting little insectivore, I suppose squeaking by with only a pretense of vampirism makes him feel more as a human.

Vlad - Exactly. Ah there you are Renfield. (Renfield comes in carrying a tray with bowls of blood...) We were just...

One - Speaking of a devil? (laughs)

Cyrule - We've just heard from Vlad of your amorous attempts to thrash a hot-blooded American vixen within an inch of her life and drain her blood to the last drop in a mind numbing orgy of blood-sucking mayhem?

Ram - Is that true Renfield? Fill in the details, let's hear about it!

Renfield - Oh no, you embarrass me. I did play with her... a little. Maybe dressing her, you know with some nice clothes... she was unconscious. I wanted to just surprise her but then I...

Cyrule - Yes?

Renfield - I touched her. (He indicates his breast and looks down.)

Vlad - You should have bitten her, not had sex! (talking slowly)

One - Sex at your age Ren, it's disgusting. But how was it, did it make you feel more like her and less of what you really are?

Renfield - I don't think I know what you mean. Here, I've brought a fine refreshment. I hope you like it master, it's still warm!

Vlad - Very good. So you've coaxed Lura back after all to donate for our little gathering?

Renfield - Not exactly.

One - What then, is the minx experiencing her death throes as we speak? Unable to control your sex crazed thirst for her life's blood you ripped at her throat with your newly grown teeth, slashing your way until even the smallest vessels yielded their precious contents into your greedy mouth. Is that it then Renfield? (laughing hoarsely)

Renfield - No, of course... not. I don't think I can say. (He leaves, going to the kitchen where the refrigerator and the groundhog tied and gagged within.)

Cyrule - Good old Renfield, what a wonder!

Vlad - Well I'm sorry to retire early. Filming starts soon and I want to be ready. You're welcome to observe at a distance for now. Make yourselves at home. Renfield has secured some guest caskets downstairs. And I had expected the usual geriatric excuses to postpone your arrival at least a night or two... (laughs and departs)

Ram - Good old Vlad, what a kidder! More like two weeks than two days since he used the signal.

One - Could be he's been resting... And just didn't bother to get a new paper so didn't realize.   (noting the old newspaper)

Ram - To sleep two weeks he must be feeding well!

One - Vlad's been busy in town, you can be sure!

2

Dracula arrives on set the next evening and is surprised they plan to shoot his scenes so early. Perhaps the schedule has been changed to accommodate the growing popularity of his first film and star status, he muses. He notices some police and men in dark suits with FBI labels are talking with a couple directors. There are also many vampire extras from Club Dracula and Guy's group in attendance. He goes over to greet them and notices that the police appear to be leaving but grudgingly, casting suspicious and hateful glances in his direction. A director takes Dracula aside...

Director - Listen we've taken care of the problem for now, but you've got to try harder to keep your private life under wraps. I know you're going to say you're just working on your character but going to crowded trendy bars and actually biting not one or two but everyone at the place in a life-threatening manner, on the neck! (He says with emphasis so others look over, then whispers...) Of course some of your friends there denied it, but look at them. They look like vampires don't they? (Vlad nods.) It's just providence the police couldn't locate you and had no choice but to come here where our accountants and attorneys were ready for them. We actually budget for this sort of thing. But after we've wrapped filming, you'll be on your own for a while! (points at him for emphasis)

3

As the police and government officials make their way off the set the director rushes over to them...

Director - You know these method actors, always bringing their work home. I bet you didn't know that Batman slept in his cape off set, Robin liked his red... jump suit. Sure (nodding) double oh seven, James Bond and his Walther PPK (pats the agent's weapon), the godfather (starts moving his jaws like he has a mouth full of cotton).

Officer - I know, stuffed cotton in his mouth in order to sound brain damaged.

Director - He did, didn't he!

Officer - Well be that as it may, we're going to have to insist that these kids (looks at Dracula's entourage of young vampires) be allowed to return to their homes. There are quite a few complaints coming in about them not returning home at night, going off to strange places... (shudders) cemeteries and defiling crypts... (director looks incredulous as if waiting to hear the punch line) sleeping in coffins! (The director throws his eyes wide open and nods, then practically pushes the government agent off the set.)

Director - And don't forget we're funding for you boys at Washington... five hundred dollars a plate. J. Edgar would be proud!

The Reemergence of Vlad!

Assistant - That's not the CIA director now.

Director - They're FBI. It doesn't matter (checks to see they've gone), they're so secret they're not supposed to know who's in charge. (assistant nods) And have those kids sent home... as long as they're not under contract! (He walks briskly to a central area, picking up a megaphone...) Okay people on your marks... (turning to Dracula) We want to start with a scene from the middle if it's alright with you, Vlad... less monotonous that way. We wouldn't want anyone to be bored and have to take a couple weeks off. (He smiles then notices Dracula intervening as the assistant tries to dismiss some of the young vampires) I see if you've been training apprentices... vampires, we may as well try them out. Never waste talent I always say, it's too hard to come by in this business! So this is a cemetery scene where you and your cohort vampires have been forewarned of a cyborg raid. Raid! (shouting... several extras from Guy's group look around startled and frantic) Just want to see who's paying attention. As you know the vampires have been dogging it with the Cyborgs at their heels. They reach their last haven on the west coast which is the Beverly Hills Memorial Park, conveniently, and where Vlad attempts to rally his demons. Remember the scene Vlad? (Dracula nods reluctantly.) Cyborgs! (shouting directions) When you find a vampire be methodical, hit them with the garlic, immobilize them with crosses and then stake through the heart but go easy and check your props.... We don't have enough insurance to cover everyone. If you've got holy water... the airline liquor bottles painted white with gold crosses, use it and later torch the coffins. But try not to destroy the set before we shoot the scene!

An Extra - What if the coffins don't burn because they're too wet?

Director – The holy water is alcohol, it'll burn but I don't want to see anyone drinking. Remember cyborgs are machines so leave the whimpers and crying in battle to the vampires. (The cyborg extras laugh and point at the vampire extras, who growl menacingly back at them.)

4

The set is a thickly wooded cemetery and set lights simulate the nearness of the dawn. The vampires take their places in crypts and graves. Dracula's entourage are also positioned about the set, some behind trees or up in the branches. The director yells *action* and the cyborgs descend over the set triggering vampire deterrents. Many vampires are quickly subdued but some react first... snatching their would be killers by the throat and setting off sparking arcs from internal circuits. Other cyborgs are flung into coffins and set ablaze. And though some vampires are being staked, others are rescued by those waiting in the trees like bats. Most the remaining cyborgs are confused by the turn of events and run off. A ranking cyborg attempting to attack Dracula is now helplessly caught in the grip of his powerful stare... only inches from his face, Dracula's eyes seem to twitch uncontrollably and glow red. His voice resounds in deep resonance...

Dracula - And when you have finished with the vampire, what next? Or have you and these computerized excuses for life forms already started killing humans? How long did it take your logical immortal minds to figure out that killing your real competition, the vampire, might lead to eliminating your other potential competition, mortal humans? (He turns to face the camera after dropping the now limp unresponsive automaton.) The less immortals left to share the world, the better. Isn't that it? The vampire kills out of physical need but for your kind it is mere sport and greed! (Dracula bares his fangs and hisses...) Be gone! (In the background the fire rescue support teams are already dousing the burning coffins and tending to injuries. The Director comes over to Dracula.)

Director - I see there's no need to yell cut! Cut! (yelling) Just in case... You really got the most out of that scene didn't you? Still, though different, it may work. We'll have to see if we had a clean angle on that last bit of footage... I don't think we can use flashing lights as a backdrop to your dramatic close-up? Or maybe we can, at this point I don't even know if I'm directing. (muttering and walking away) Am I directing? (to assistant) God I wish I knew how he does those effects... We're going to have to give him his script changes if he can keep coming up with stuff like that! Those eyes! I've never seen anything like it... (The assistant nods. The Director turns back and takes Vlad over to the side for a talk...) That'll be all we need from you tonight Vlad. We'll just be taking some scenery shots and maybe a few setups with extras for tomorrow's action... By the way, the action shots may start to get a little rough, are you sure you don't want any stunt men?

Vlad - Yes quite sure. I don't want to be misinterpreted by the audience.

Director - I see, very good. Well if you change your mind just let me know. We'll have somebody on call! (patting Vlad as he departs... then softly to the special effects man) I want you to rig up those explosions pretty strong.

I think he can take it. Anyway don't worry about it, the movie isn't about a vampire role model slash hero! Maybe he'll get the message... eventually.

No one seems to notice that several gaunt impressive looking figures wearing leather tunics, complete with cloak and cape follow Vlad as he departs the set...

5

Dracula and his guests are relaxing at his stately old home and discussing the new trends of vampirism... for one, how sleeping in an earth filled coffin is no longer in vogue.

Ram - It's true, a garment bag is easily unrolled and placed either above or below the mattress, and can hold plenty of dirt close enough for a restful sleep!

One - Yes the old ways are just a metaphor to some now... A coffin is becoming as passe' as a simple security measure... that of the smallest possible refuge. The lessons they say imparted from the old habits are... obsolete, and a coffin is only as good as the crypt it is kept in. Some of the new ones even advocate vitamins to break the addiction... to coffins.

Vlad - What of our image? For the sake of legend... people knowing of the vampire's fondness for heavy coffins has instilled a kind of fear, the stark reminder of death! The living will always strive to avoid its proximity... the thought that a weighty coffin lid bearing down on them someday just as surely as the sun will rise sets them running. It has to be. I can't believe that this group of all vampires should forget our ways. Your powers could be diminished!

Ram - Times change, interests change... You yourself prefer a plush er large house... There are other things in death aside from powers, aren't there? No one takes us very seriously anymore anyway. You can thank your Hollywood for that, don't blame us! Though some of the high budget films with better effects can be flattering now and then.

Cyrule - I especially liked the Tom Cruise and Brad Pitt depictions as a world travelers, lovers of arts, culture and music, in addition to possessing the cunning wit of ruthless murderers. (laughs) Interview with a Vampire! (Ha.) Compelling, that one!

One – I'm afraid I go for that old standby, the mystery... vampire detective shows! Who better than the vampire to use his prodigious powers in aiding the forces of good, and the NYPD. And such a fetching name as well, 'Forever Knight' with a 'K.' My favorite.

Ram - Oh I like the one about the British Highlander who works on his own like a private eye and does away with old comrades gone bad with neat and just beheadings. (feeling his throat) Thrilling.

One - He gets a charge out of killing quite literally as might a vampire! Well Vlad there have been some other changes, most notably dealing with religion... some of us have even joined churches! Or so they've claimed.

Ram - Yes with all the new confusion and uncertainty, you find yourself needing to believe in something with more meaning... than just mere existence, however long it may be. You know many vampires have turned to traditional faiths.

Cyrule - Some of the young priests are so eloquent and persuasive... There are a couple of churches downtown that I've heard are fabulous Vlad. I'll leave a reference for you with the elders.

Vlad - What are you talking about, we're the only elders... 'You *are* the elders,' (talking sarcastically, mimicking his voice) How can you let yourselves be taken in by religious charlatans after all these centuries? They're just mortals, for God's sake!

Ram - Of course as you might expect there were some bad experiences. Armand was lost before his conversion to Christianity. Seems he decided to attend a sunrise communion service. (Cyrule chuckles, the others shake their heads.)

Vlad - Armand?

One - That was his Christian name. You'd know him as Grendel, the ancient evil.

Vlad - (shaking his head) Well he's been killed before. He survived the slaying by Beowulf back at the dawn of civilization and many others since.

Cyrule - But this time it was self-inflicted.

Vlad - I just don't believe it.

One - Unfortunately he's not the only one to meet with accident. Horace was caught in a storm while flying at sea in the tropics. It quickly developed into a hurricane with 150 mile an hour winds that forced him to travel within the eye for days until he realized he could fly out above the storm. He survived the storm but was hunted down for dining on an entire island's inhabitants recklessly when he returned.

The Reemergence of Vlad!

Vlad - Hermes, Aphrodite, Athena, Caesar! Where are they who have ruled countries, even the known world several times over, and choose for their names those of the early gods? The topics of countless legends, sculpture, art and general ill will... gone? Have they been tracking the Marcos gold perhaps? Or cornering the market on poppy seeds? Or merely undermining some government for the thrill of it, maybe they've gone to Russia or the Middle East? What has sheer boredom driven them to this time?

One - The pit of hell it seems... All are finally at eternal peace with themselves we're sad to say. Yes... all gone in merely a flash. 'Happened at a meeting in Hawaii, and since its purpose was less than purposeful they hadn't bothered to contact you...' Naturally, knowing your level headed nature of late. Well they were using the purest strain of drugs from a South American drug lord, and in amounts that would have killed entire armies... Rumor is they entranced themselves playing at a game guessing the dimensions of an active volcano or its intensity, sheer foolishness. Daring themselves further and further, the party descended on the wing into the fiery abyss. Of course just as they neared the surface of the lava pool a huge flare erupted as an errant solar flare of the sun might occur, sucking them to their doom. Perhaps one day they'll be unearthed by archaeologists similar to the citizens of Pompeii and their ashes spread to the winds.

Ram - Or maybe they were saved by Vulcan, the god of fire, just before the end? (looking at One)

One - There was nothing that could be done and now that they're truly gone, I'm not above saying that their passions rarely climbed above frivolous passions... By the way I was able to get it on video tape.

Vlad - Now whose passions are misplaced? (pauses) If they are truly gone I might be inclined to agree, but they have lived through so many burnings and dismemberments before. I'll never forget Caesar's account when formerly as Herod he allowed himself to be murdered by his own family seven different ways simultaneously, and later as a young Caesar drawn and quartered behind enemy lines. A feat of survival that may have helped him become Emperor. Then of course brutally stabbed by friend and foe alike in an orgy of blood on the very steps of the Senate, possibly the most famous murder in history!

Cyrule - He was a wonder!

Vlad - They may have experienced life and death to the fullest passion, but always returned to the earth of their birth with head and heart intact...

One - A pleasing sentiment Vlad. It's at times like these I'd rather all the young ones be kept mortals, influenced and weak... undeserving as they are. Here take a look at this. (He leaves the room briefly and returns with a video player. The fiery deaths of the old vampires are replayed for Dracula... He muses.)

Cyrule - You know the reason that One doesn't want a name? He's a number because he won't play a character in history... Let the younger ones have the fun he says.

Ram - One's a wonder. (He looks at One.)

Vlad - Soon they'll be no vampires playing roles... Nature has finally caught us and now begins the struggle to survive! But what of Pluto? He was always bright and perceptive, contrary to name. Where is he?

Ram - I heard he became impatient with modern commercialism and the new mechanized way of life. Then 'sought enlightenment with the Buddhist faith...

Vlad - What of it?

Ram - Well he was counseled to trek across a Himalayan mountain with the barest essentials. It's rumored he swore an oath against his powers and then proceeded to fall into a steep crevice where he's become part of a glacier that could last a million years!

Vlad - You see how religion can warp the mind? I hope it wasn't intentional, but I doubt he'll come to his senses frozen in a block of ice...

One - So Vlad, before you decide that we should commit war against mankind for the loss of our ageless comrades... Why is it, you've summoned us?

Vlad - War on mankind? No, what would we be without them? Their little worlds, their cities, even pastimes, the television... movies! It is about my small movie of great proportion of course...

Cyrule - Perhaps many small movies once you're a star, eh Vlad? Would you be a star playing roles, or playing the role of star? Only his fans will know!

Vlad - (ignoring Cyrule) Rather than allowing humans to go on in their way... without us, I've decided that it may be time to make available our gift, eternal life to a greater number... those who would be ready to receive it.

One - You don't say!

Ram - Your kidding, that's never been our way... Don't you remember the crusading Christians, the middle ages and what they called us... heathens, devils, abominations... All those things! It's been so long now, but they did so many things to break our spirits and make us feel like outcasts. And the killing!

You can't forget what it's like to hear a vampire scream! Caskets dug up and dragged out, thrown open to the light... wooden stakes thudding through weakened flesh.... those hideous screams!

Cyrule - Besides we only bite what we need or can handle, more vampires would just compound the problem.

One - So to reach them on that scale, you'd use your movie as an advertisement?

Vlad - A vehicle of necessity... Soon the world may no longer be enough for us... It is time to break the shackles of darkness and awake the human mind to the reality of their situation and what we have to offer... They may accept, at least those with reason. Second and more importantly, if we don't win enough converts to swell our ranks we may soon be outdone by the likes of those only hinted at in the movie... another breed of immortal! (They are aghast.) And one that may hunt us down for sport as thoroughly as Christians in Rome, the Jews in Germany...

One - American Indians? Witches in Salem? Vampires in the Crusades? Ram, I realize every vampire has his tale of persecution, but I really hadn't heard you'd had it that bad!

Ram - Anywhere but a sanctified church cemetery simply wasn't safe.

One - So in the movie it is the Crusades revisited, and these cyborgs are... real? Are you sure it may not be just a small purging for the excesses of the past?

Ram – The crusades may have been the worst, but the Christians have always deserved their abuse... mocking us with their communion ritual, drinking their symbolic blood, making light of our weakness. Could the cyborg threat then make Christians seem trivial in comparison?

Vlad - If the indications of what I've learned are true, what may come someday soon could be much worse than a purging. Not only would they be as immortal as we... They wouldn't be bothered by any weakness! The subtle nuisances a vampire confronts and which can at times plague or subdue him mean nothing to these brutes.

One – (trying to change the subject) Is it my imagination or is garlic becoming a much more popular household spice? Garlic flavored everything, or I am I just paranoid...

Ram – (playing along) When you think about it things really weren't so good even in Roman times. Everyone worshiped the sun, the city was a cemetery at night. Sure they had lamps and sorts of lighting, especially the wealthy, but the quality... The social calender for a vampire was nearly limited to the invasion of dreams and nightmares! Almost all rose with the day!

Cyrule - You have to admit, with their love for tunics and togas, they knew how to dress though. No one could master the art of draping a cape around a body like the Romans. Something any cloak wearing vampire should appreciate! There were even laws the regarding the ways to wear them, remember?

Vlad - Have I brought you here to reminisce about the fashions two thousand years ago while our future is at stake?

One – (sidestepping Vlad) You have to admit, some things were better then weren't they? More often than not an inept barber would be condemned as a vampire for leaving his mark on a neck. And their rituals of superstition! The only thing easier than invading their dreams was to drive them mad with reality. There was always some epidemic of bloodsucking animal!

Vlad – Yes, who could forget, but it's time to use our wits again! Now we must convince modern Americans that what might otherwise be considered the acts of nightly foraging animals is really the work of our *army* of vampires!

One – (ignoring Vlad) And when they had exterminated the last viper, they still believed they were under imminent threat! For indeed they were! But *now* we are to announce our presence, that *we* intend to save the pitiable human race and end their suffering at the hands of these cyborg creatures before it has even begun?

Vlad – *Yesss...* Again it will be as if invading their dreams.... These movies will implant the desire to seek vampirism from the threat of mechanized men they know will come! But we still need *something* else to succeed, a kind of insurance policy. Where's Armageddon? He always has a ready plan, equal to just about any challenge. I was looking forward to his input.

One - Yes, another casualty I'm afraid but possibly just missing...

Ram - Remember what an amazing job he did stirring up a frenzy of fanaticism over the use of gunpowder... how he thought it would usher in the golden age of *vampirism* with about half the population of the world in a constant state of bleeding bliss from their wounds... He wasn't far wrong.

One - Now he's been missing some half century... It was rumored he may have been one of the first to contact a race of otherworldly aliens in the American Midwestern desert, a place called Roswell, in the early 1950's. He'd been telling of fantastic visits of rather inferior creatures in superior aircrafts and how he had always wanted to contact a race of the third kind, something neither human nor vampire... and I guess he may have. I just hope he had time to bring some of his homeland's soil and a sturdy coffin or two for any extended trips.

Vlad - Uh yes, truly remarkable.

Ram - Aliens! What next? Sometimes I miss the simpler days, don't you? Back when people only worried about whether their priests could predict the seasons or the occasional roving murderer on the prowl...

Vlad - That's pretty far back isn't it even before the Christians, but murderers have always been rather commonplace.

Ram - Back when most people were wanderers, before cities... just wandering here and there with their animals and waiting to be attacked by a wolf or vampire. They expected it, even took it in stride. 'Almost an *alien* world when compared with today, with everyone expecting basic human rights, and *police* everywhere! Do you know that now they have these stun guns that shoot electric rays thirty feet... invisible rays, can you believe it? You get hit with that and you feel it in your teeth, needless to say a sensitive area. (Says shuddering.) A shot of mace to the face, just passé these days. (pauses) Maybe it would serve Arm right to have been abducted. The world may become a saner place. I could have done without his obsession with gunpowder, and the insane race for arms that ensued... The times I've been under weapons fire, it's not the kind of thing I've enjoyed keeping track of...

Vlad - Yes well he's been shot as well, as we all have, everyone suffers the pangs of progress and guns would be here regardless. This is different. It's crazy to think we'd be any better off without guns... Primitive hostility is human nature. 'Transforming the entire race is another matter. Some vampires always manage to let themselves be clubbed down, some later to find they've been staked or beheaded. How do you think man first learned our weaknesses? We certainly didn't sit around bragging at local Inns!

Cyrule - Don't be to sure about that!

Vlad - But we should be plotting our action, not this drunken storytelling...

One - Speaking of which, I could use another tall one as long as Renfield's not bleeding himself. That other had something of a peculiar flavor...

Cyrule - Where's your wonderful housekeeper Vlad, and more importantly his blood supply? (Renfield appears with goblets of blood, grinning insanely...)

Ram - We can drink to death. (They raise their glasses in a silent toast to departed comrades.)

Vlad - You're right our friends deserve their due. Maybe we should lament a while and debate their honor... We might consider how it can be that their passing causes not even a ripple in the sea of humanity. Shouldn't lives of such extent and wonder be raised up again from the dead to be remembered, even worshiped as they did for the character Jesus? Answer me that?

Ram - It isn't a vampires way, even in death... too much instinctual drive for self preservation. We've always relied on stealth to avoid detection.

Cyrule – (ignoring Ram) Vampires arise from their deaths to exist as undead much as the Christ arose as only a brief prelude to apparent eternal nothingness. Now you've got me nagging on about the Christians!

Vlad – (seizing on his favorite topic) And if possessing such great importance, has no one vampire or human encountered him since? The world is mad! The truth stares them in the face and they prefer a two thousand year fable.

The Reemergence of Vlad!

Ram - Maybe he's a better vampire than any, even we!

Vlad – Perhaps he is the consummate vampire, never having been heard from or seen...

One - But at least you're older Vlad. (He smiles and shrugs his shoulders.) It's too bad none of us had known him personally. You might have divined the true reason for his greatness. I propose that he was very well liked and as such chosen to be a symbol to oppose a hopelessly corrupt society. His followers probably felt they had no alternative but to hype the event of his death as a spectacular miracle, to get back at his executioners and society in general. And as a martyr he even became still more a hero because now his enemies were fighting the memory of his life... an opponent with no substance, a ghost?

Vlad - Perhaps, because other than their virtue the Christian stories of wild miracles were not much more exciting than those of other Roman gods. But when the Emperors began claiming god status for themselves they made their whole system too far fetched. Still it could have been the vampire stories of those days that might have risen to prominence instead.

One - If you ask me a miracle occurs anytime a large enough group of people pass a story from one another. Fantastic things are always added for spice or whatever reason... Regarding this particular Christian, Jesus, I may not have met him but I did hear first hand the stories from some of his followers around the time of the Resurrection story. Some said the male followers were too afraid when Jesus died so the women were the only ones to come to his grave at first, a simple nearby cave. There the women met James, Jesus' younger brother, dressed as Jesus himself in order to frighten potential robbers that might want to steal the body in order to later sell it back to the church as a shrine to the young faith. Either these first visitors then buried him or the body was actually stolen and buried, but then never recovered. Anyway with James' brief appearances performing in the manner and speech of his brother he thought to energize the frightened followers and prevent the collapse of the faith Jesus had worked so hard to build up. Some of the less savory followers who knew parts of the truth attempted to ransom the body to Roman officials but were apparently not told the correct grave site. They were among the first Christians to meet the lions in the new coliseum. If they'd been smart though they would have sought their buyers among the higher pagan nobility or the Emperor himself, then they might have been spared or possibly even expose the whole scheme. (One adjusts the hem on his garment.) They might have been killed regardless, you know how it was... sometimes the gods were angered, sometimes not. You might be executed if you happened to be a slave for the sport of it at the coliseum. After all Jesus himself was sentenced for overturning a few tables... a matter of attitude, not liking his accountants!

Dracula - (smiling) With your ear for a story I'm going to see if they can make room for you on the writing staff. The movie is constantly overlooking the vampire viewpoint.

Cyrule - He will for a price!

One - (massaging Vlad's shoulder) Ease up Vlad, ease up. It's been two thousand years hasn't it? I hardly think your Jesus is something worth worrying about now.

Dracula - Don't you? When you realize what I have in mind, what I hope to achieve with my movie, my influence! The two thousand year anniversary of the Christian Resurrection is not without significance. For all we know a new miracle will arrive eclipsing the less desirable vampire *legends* for another thousand years!

Ram - Hey I'll show you a miracle I've been working on... (He takes a deep breath exhaling out a white cloud of which emerges the shape of a young naked girl beckoning to them. A moment later it's gone. They laugh except Vlad, still looking serious.) I've been practicing that one, great for getting someone off his guard at four in the morning on a dark lonely street... (They laugh again except Vlad.)

Vlad - I feel these cyborgs will be our greatest nightmare.

One - Nightmare, daymare, daymare, dahmer... Listen Vlad, I've heard it before. Science fiction wasn't born yesterday you know. They've been dreaming up those things since the fifteenth century, and Leo da Vinci!

Vlad - Most of us here now know the futility of war with its addictive thirst for power, and the ultimate vengeful revolts of conquered people... Now we may soon be the conquered, but if we are ready we may be the first to avoid disaster.

One – And thus be the winners? (he laughs)

Vlad - (passing around newspaper clippings of scientific breakthroughs) Take a look at these articles. (Headlines read... Chinese Breakthrough in Android Microcomputer Technology, Man's Genes Mapped - What Next?, Experimental Immortality Achieved with Amphibian Nerve Cells, Cyborgs... Man or Machine - You Decide!) There's no doubt the technology is advanced and available and there will soon be an emergence of a new immortality, aside from frogs. Whether it will be as the movie predicts I'm not sure, but I'm certain it'll happen. It's been five thousand years since a wheel was fashioned to fit a chariot's hub, the only purpose to defeat a neighboring tribe. (There's a sudden scuffling at the door, then in strides a slender dark complexioned man in a tight fitting black tunic decorated with gold... arm bands, bracelets, belts and a turquoise pendant.)

Visitor - Are we going to let ourselves be overrun? Outdone? Upstaged? No! We must join battle and enter the fray first with our weapons drawn! Make ourselves known for who we are, the Pharaoh's own immortal elite! And what must we do? Retake the Nile Delta for all time before it's too late! (He laughs at the stunned silence...) Wasn't that the speech I gave before my battle with Persia opposing a youthful ruler by the name of Cyrus or Cyrule? Something like that... (Cyrule comes up and claps him on the back.)

Cyrule - Come and sit down, you old dog from hell! Before we call the Bureau of Antiquities and have them drag you back to your precious Egypt!

Vlad - Yes Osiris! Good of you to come... I thought there'd been someone listening at the door.

One - Sounds like something I might have said as well in Rome and again in Carthage and to a young lad, Alexander... before he was great and deciding to leave home that first time... (musing) He could barely master tying his own tunic!

Osiris - We simply don't believe you, don't bother going on about it. Sheesh!

One – (glaring at Osiris) You don't have to wear gold or royal purple to tell war stories. (Cyrule shifts uncomfortably.) So then Vlad (ignoring Osiris) you've decided it's time for the next Jesus, Buddha, Mohammad, what have you... to lead the humans to salvation. Is that it? And that you're elected?

Osiris - What his 'Oneness' is trying to say is that he doesn't think it's going to fly Vlad. (smiling at One) But of course his is only *One* opinion...

Ram - Maybe Vlad thinks it's time for another all out war on Christianity... Who can forget, speaking of Rome, that fevered excitement in the years after Jesus was killed? And how Vlad got himself into the thick of it... joining the night games at the huge new coliseum, becoming the star gladiator against his better judgment! Terminus your name, wasn't it? Killing and maiming Christians in every possible way: lion tossing, drowning, torching, neck biting the specialty of course... You could see him literally reeking in jealousy for their faith in a dead King, disgusting. And then finally banished for missing an important day game. (laughs)

Vlad - Yes but by then I was wealthy with noble status. It was just that stupid Nero and his whim that had me banished. You know he only killed Christians out of convenience, when he was short of other spectacles to show. He didn't care much about them one way or another but somehow managed to ensnare their new leader, Paul... and blamed him for starting the great fire in Rome. Ha! Fire starting was the only excuse he could ever think of for an execution! 'That due to his own famed addiction to pyromania...

One – Well I remember that what you'd started turned out to be bad times for Christians and vampires alike! There was so much confusion that anyone found hiding during the day was thought to be one. Crucifixions and beheadings were pretty efficient against us as well. Thank God they were usually too busy to attend to those things right away and some could make their escape by nightfall. Many were weak though having been imprisoned by day and died carrying their crosses or at the public trials. I'd seen vampires even crucified at night then stabbed with sharp poles to be sure... there wasn't much that could be done.

Osiris - And by following the spear men you would hardly want for blood, would you One? (One stares again, eyes glowing greenish.)

Cyrule - Those were heady days alright. I guess we can't blame Vlad and his need to erupt into the limelight from time to time having lived through that. Or any of us!

Ram - But Christians were scarcely the only sect sharing the stigma of hatred and evil with vampires. Maybe we survive today more from our ties to religions than our fear of it? Is it coincidence that a Muslim may not eat or drink during daylight hours in the month of Ramadan, my namesake? Muslims make their way to Mecca, a holy city to which they must return, as a vampire is not without the earth of his birthplace... Just as our own Vlad has practiced mass exterminations of Christians and other enemies, Castle Dracula for instance, the fourteenth century, when he placed thousands on large vertical spikes.... Muslims, Christians and many other religions have often purged the world of non-believers though there will probably never be a religion that can lay equal claim to Vlad's flare for decadence! And what of the Buddhists? (Vlad regards him stonily.) In Buddhism an evil Buddhist must undergo changes in form, reincarnation, sometimes many phases depending on their degree of evilness in order to reach the highest plane of paradise, nirvana. Again what vampire doesn't enjoy the bliss of transformation? (Renfield has been standing near the kitchen entrance but now quietly slinks from their midst.) The unavoidable association vampires share with evil is worrisome...

that all vampires are inherently evil? Or perhaps the evil of one has influenced the fortunes of the rest?

Vlad - I hope you're not trying to imply anything. And why is it of all the events of our considerable past you always speak of that time. I spend centuries forgetting but I can count on you to bring up Rome, Transylvania, the Inquisition? So you want to think of the prospect of heaven or nirvana, but you should ask yourself if that's what you really want! Ram, you'd give up unending existence for a tenuous uncertain situation at best. And then of course you'd have to give up taunting me... If you're worried I might lose control and rampage, *don't*. I have more help this time and give me credit for having learned a few things since last we met.

Ram - Being hunted countless centuries as disciples of Dracula does provide that consolation... survival instinct.

Vlad - So your little speech on comparative religion degenerates to whining babble blaming me for your problems. Typical. If you want to just sit back and ignore the problem, hoping the years might push it away, you may. But when the new immortals come and they will, they'll be the ones superior and ready to hunt us down. This time may be the last!

Cyrule - I suggest then we employ the tactics of the Roman Imperial Guard! Sensing our potential enemy to at some point become a threat, we pounce early, crushing them completely! It worked with Carthage!

One - I recall that Rome eventually paid dearly for that aggression, many would say deservedly. But that's hardly a lesson to be learned by conquerors! (Cyrule shakes his head.)

Vlad - Though these are modern times, we face the deaths of all. It may only be a few short years if science continues at this rate.

Osiris - We're with you Vlad. One is just trying to be the sissy Mary, every group has one. (They look at One and snicker.) And Ram, named for an outdated month! What kind of fame is that? (Ram hisses.)

Ram - Tell us what we can do Vlad.

6

Vlad discusses scenes in the movie and their roles. Later that night he outlines the basic psychology of their approach.

Vlad - Ram has already pointed out that the similarities between major religions, especially Christianity, and vampirism are highly suspect. It is of course born out of intense feelings of jealousy, rivalry and the desire to be on an even keel with us, their earthly gods. Since the only way to influence the masses is through what they hold most dear, their religion, we will show them that they have in fact been worshiping us for thousands of years and the illusion is over. We'll let them experience some miracles, real salvation granted as new vampires are created on screen for all to see... a sacrament of blood, actual resurrection from death. It's sure to sway their sentiments! Once we have the focus of their souls we can begin to attack the new science. How could the two be compared... the human mind encoded onto worthless metallic hardware, and the fantastic miracle of the vampire, the highest form of existence! There need be no more false shrines and altars, no holy city of

The Reemergence of Vlad!

Jerusalem, no Meccas, no divine inner peace but their own coffins! This time we'll rock religion to its core, the only zealots left will be those believing in an intelligent design to the universe, and it'll be our intelligence! Vampirism!

One - Vlad you could really pass for one of the preachers you despise so much. I can see you behind the pulpit, eyes blazing and hissing, the congregation frozen from fear!

Vlad - I might, on the behalf of vampires, for vampirism.

Cyrule - So we're here then to help you spread the word, is that it?

Vlad - (sighing) Something like that.

Ram - I was afraid of that, That's not our way is it, One?

Vlad - Yes but there are things you can do that are... a vampire's way.

Ram, One, Cyrule, Osiris – Yes...

One – We know what you mean Vlad.

Osiris - I think we can think of some way to help... (licking the tips of his teeth)

Vlad - Tomorrow you'll meet the directors and make some movie magic, even a star needs co-stars... even Dracula! (They smile.) We will let the audience see for themselves the choices that lay before them.

One - I suppose it's cedar and mothballs for us again then. (He glances at the cellar door considering the next day's rest.)

Osiris - Don't bother about a coffin for me, I've brought my own. Next day air service is great isn't it? (He opens the front door and brings in a simply decorated Egyptian sarcophagus.) I always prefer my traveling sarcophagus! (They laugh, but stop when Osiris lets his sarcophagus crash down the stairs...) Don't worry, solid metal. Much more manageable than stone!

Vlad - That may be but the others are wood! (They join him at the top of the stairs. Osiris snaps his fingers in acknowledgment of his mistake. They file downstairs and Renfield comes out of hiding to tidy up the main room.)

7

On the movie set the next evening. Vlad has engaged an opposing cyborg in battle.

Vlad - When you have been killed as often in battle on the field of honor as I or if at least your enemies believe they have rendered you so with their own hands, then you will know the futility of what you do. (opponent looks puzzled)

Opponent - If that's true, I'd think that would be one honor you could do without. Maybe you should consider discretion... You know, as the better part of a valorless death when facing such superior opponents?

Vlad – Discretion, valor... mere words on the field of battle. Though I admit to considering them more often of late, where modern governments are concerned. (The cyborg actor appears dazed, not following the lines.) In this instance however I fight for a high cause against a low... opponent. And the only thing superior about you will be the depth of your wounds.

Opponent - What? (Before he can protest Dracula's ad lib further Dracula has dealt the actor a mortal blow with his dagger. The effect is actually hypnotic but seems very real.) That's not part of the... (the opponent falls)

The Reemergence of Vlad!

Vlad - (cleaning off the blade) A little trick I picked up from a previous co-star...

8

Off stage a director and assistant are talking.

Asst. Director - The word from the hospital is that they think two of the cyborg actors may be in comas, something about not being able to stop the bleeding. (Director looks over for a moment toward the actor Vlad's just stabbed to be sure he's still moving.) Although they're hoping it could be hysterical paralysis, psychological. Worse is that the extras, in particular the good guys, the humans and cyborgs... the nonvampires...

Director - I know who the good guys are!

Asst. Director - Yes well they've all got neck bites! (he adds quickly) They're not sure how it happened but there's an idea the...

Director - (eyes wide) The vampires got them!?

Asst. Director - And not only the actors, half the production staff, camera crew, stagehands, lighting, everyone... (talking very fast) I think we've got to wrap up very soon, imagine what that many lawsuits could do!

Director - Put us out on our cans... that's what. (assistant starts sobbing) Hardgrave'll have a tantrum! Well there are still enough extras left to do the big scene, ready or not. If we have to, we can use the outtakes later for fillers, nobody'll notice.

Asst. Director - Then we'll send everyone home?

Director - (talking to himself) This scene better work! (goes over to talk to Vlad) Don't think I don't know what you're trying to pull. You may have artistic license but I also have final say... And the producers have already told me what to say! You and those cronies of yours only get one chance at the war scene. Let's see you act your way out of this one!

Vlad - My acquaintances may be relishing their roles more than you'd like but it is in the movie's best interest, I assure you.

Director - Okay people (loudly to others) let's go! We're doing one more scene and then that's it! (loud cheering from cast and crew) There's the budget, we're out of time... my sick aunt in Idaho who you don't want to know about. (weak cheers) I know you're tired, you all look pale, weak... a little moldy about the gills. You don't have to tell me. (moaning, some faint) But believe it or not this is an important project, a high concept picture! This is something usually feared and generally avoided by Hollywood, but we're going to be one of the exceptions, aren't we? (muffled cheers, some coughs) So the producers want the premise put to the people! Excuse the alliteration... What we have is the very real likelihood of a future controlled by mechanized projections of ourselves, the cyborgs! (cheers from the cyborg actors) The future probably also holds some miraculous possibilities for human longevity as well but only with new and unusual drawbacks in aberrant science, the latter naturally represented by the vampire. (scattered applause by the cyborgs, some vampires hiss...) We've been trying to show the only way we can... through extensive makeup and special effects that the cyborgs (laughing by vampires) have been imbued with personality, memory... the very souls of their human counterparts. (booing vampires) We all know the quintessential challenge of any great actor is the portrayal of soul. (He scans the cast with a hard expression.) Unfortunately up to now this has been an action picture... guns, bombs, sneak attacks, some limited pillaging, and a few rapes. And contrary to the script the vampires have been getting the upper hand. (cheers from vampires) Though we do have some good special effects footage of Vlad being shot and blown up at the same time... (The actors look at Vlad and he shrugs nonchalantly.)

Anyway tonight all manner of torture has been designed for the vampires with the future of society at stake. Cyborgs, you'll be killing like there's no tomorrow. Remember there's nothing more intrinsic to the human soul than the killer instinct. You'll also be rescuing the cattle, (coughs) or the humans from vampire bondage! (The cast seems bored.) So the vampires have shown us they're tough, all the more reason they should be killed in the roughest possible ways! Places everyone! (shouting)

9

The scene is set on a small artificial hill with a backdrop of a large sprawling community in the distant valley. Vlad is talking with One. It's twilight, the stars are bright.

One - So it comes to this then, Vlad... herding the last remnants of humanity for our sustenance and their protection? They deplete their numbers to become cyborgs faster than we can make them vampires.

Vlad - While the mountain of cyborg scrap carcasses grows daily. All a waste.

One - Do you suppose it was the marketing, the sexual hype? Sex is always a good sell...

Vlad - Possibly.

One - Their scientific breakthroughs in levels of sustained animatronic pleasure circuitry... (Vlad frowns) promising a multiplicity of orgasmic potential, ever greater plateaus of sensation, until reaching the nirvana-like state of mind, if a robot could have a real mind... Whereas vampires have the reputation of never mating and delivering more pain than pleasure... except for foreplay of course! (One smiles somewhat psychotically)

Vlad - The problem is probably even more basic. Vampires exist too far afield from the sphere of normalcy for human comprehension... thinking we exist only by night, rigid confinement to coffins, the constant unredeemable conflict with organized religion, and other excruciating weaknesses... the association with other forms of animal, bats, dogs. It's too much for most of them.

One - Where is the church when they turn themselves into metal, synthetics? They'd fought hard to prevent abortions and now they don't conceive! The last vestige of their humanity taken!

Director - (looking concerned) That's not in the script! (says tersely under his breath) *None* of it is!

One - (continuing) Only in theory, their science promises births of an infinity of random personalities and neural patterns. But as yet, untried! They're so busy building cyborgs for immediate conversion they've no time for adequate testing.

Vlad - It's to their ultimate loss they're so concerned with annihilating the vampire. Maybe if enough of them can survive, when this cyborg threat is done, then someday they will learn.

Ram - (arrives at their side, flying in rapidly on huge wings) Vlad, One, the attack comes! The oldest are ready and in their places. I hope this will be the last. (He spreads the great webbed wings and flies a little further along the ridge.)

10

At that moment thunderous artillery and laser beamed weapons fire. A queer assortment of mechanized war vehicles and cyborgs in heavy armor crest the hill and begin firing at Vlad and One. The vampires move quickly and appear to blur or vanish, seeming to be several places at once. Other vampires converge on the scene, some distracting, others leading cyborgs to ambush. Wings fill the sky. The cyborg infantry is methodically attacked, armor plates and panels are pried off exposing vulnerable hardware... or necks broken to disengage helpless head electronics. More experienced vampires use hypnotic stares causing cyborgs to fire on each other. Small groups of vampires surround tanks with deceptive clouds of mist and appear as multiples to draw the fire of other tanks. Vlad and Osiris seemingly morph into the dragons of old spewing fire and white heat across the battlefield melting the remaining vehicles and trapping cyborgs within molten blocks of metal. As the smoke subsides Vlad and One are again standing together. Ram on flapping wings signals to them...

Ram - Depart! We've activated their explosives to detonate in minutes. The blast could be strong!

11

Soon they are all flying high in the skies while the ground erupts in a volcanic upheaval of rock, fire, vehicles, props... and cyborgs.

Director- It's not too late to stop, is it? (talking weakly and looking at the scene... incredulous, not believing the destruction) Did the cameras get it all, not that I'm going to use it understand? (starts twitching, looking maniacal, then yells) Did they get it?!

Film Crew Chief - (gives the thumbs up that it was filmed in entirety) All cameras accounted for!

Director - Will someone get me some coffee here! (yelling at the top of his lungs)

A messenger runs up to Vlad telling him the director wants to talk with him right away, the other vampires depart, most flying off. The messenger watches with amazement.

The Reemergence of Vlad!

Director - I thought that was special effects. (Then he notices cyborg actors limping from the area, many remaining on the set motionless or moaning.)

Vlad – You called for me?

Director - Have a seat in my new office. (They are at the wilderness backdrop of the destroyed set.) This is where my office will be. You'll like being outdoors, they'll say. (looking away) I don't know if you realize you've done it but you've completely changed the ending! And none of those lines were from the script! Still it came off well, maybe better than if the good guys had won... I know you want to be the hero, bringing in your friends from the old country was it? (coughs) I won't deny the stunts were impressive... some famous Transylvanian circus? (holds up his hand) No, I don't want to know.

Vlad - I am sorry about the script. The movie will have more relevance later, you'll see. I must go. (turns and departs)

Director - (mimicking) I must go... (talking to himself though the assistant is nearby) Vlad wants things his way; he stages a coup d'etat and wins because he has friends and special powers. The producers will say the actors always want things their way, that's nothing new. We hired you to do things our way. Then I say... but they wouldn't listen because... (long pause, then to assistant) Maybe the effects people can touch it up. You know, make the vampires look like cyborgs and visa versa. Yeah just go in for close ups of expressions then pan way back for the action? (He makes a pathetic face.)

Assistant - Maybe if we hired a staff of animators... (shaking his head) But that would be more work than completely reshooting and we're already over budget. Plus I don't think we can get those stunts again...

Director - Why not?

Assistant - Well there have been some injuries. A lot of cyborg men seem to be hurt, some badly. The ambulances have been called. Those not injured in stunts have been bitten... again!

Director - Bitten?

Assistant - (showing his neck wounds) Everyone is ill... At first I didn't notice. I thought it might be our nightly schedule that left me feeling desperately tired during the day, or maybe cancer you know? Then I noticed these. (massages his neck) The worst is not knowing... if I enjoyed it. (winks at Director)

Director - I give up! Look I'll call the insurance people in the morning. Go home and rest. If anybody asks, tell them it's over. I'll be at Betty Ford's if someone needs me. (They leave as the ambulances arrive at the set. The assistant points toward the casualties.)

12

The next evening, it's still dusk when Renfield answers the door.

Renfield - No, no. You mustn't! (talking to unseen messenger) Please stay back. I'm warning you. I will lay down my life!

Messenger - Okay, okay. I'll let you sign. Just take the damn letter! (He shoves a letter in Renfield's hand and leaves, letting Renfield keep the pen. Moments later Dracula emerges and sees Renfield with the letter before putting it away.

Dracula - (hisses)   Another postman Renfield?   (says emotionally, keeping a keen eye for his servant's response)

Renfield - Yes master and very persistent.

Dracula - (taking letter) I don't like it... News crews are one thing, gawking fans another, but it is the postman I detest. They have the backing of the federal government you know Renfield, that makes them think they are unstoppable.

Renfield - Yes but he didn't get in this time. Don't worry.

Dracula - Well (reading the letter) electric fences may be a good idea. We have guests now after all. (He turns to face Ram and One seated nearby.)

Renfield - Yes, is it about the movie? (looking furtively to the others)

Dracula - From the producers in fact... it seems my considerable donations of money and talent are not enough for them. Something about compensation for breaking the contract, unsanctioned changes, unreasonable injuries to everyone connected with the set except vampire actors... the deductibles on the insurance claims for stunt men alone will cost tens of thousands. Inevitable suits for loss of work, incurable disease... a lot of extra work for publicists... will require the royalties be withheld, etc, etc, etc.

One - It takes the fun right out of being a vampire doesn't it? Legalities and contracts are just newer forms of slavery in the modern world.

Ram - You can't fight city hall Vlad. Impassioned revolts only happen in the movies these days... not like in the middle ages. You can't throw the royals out on their ears... on a whim. (Vlad ignores him momentarily.)

Vlad - And if I don't comply with this dispute (waving letter) they promise to have the dialog dubbed over on the scenes we just shot. (reading) Extra footage of dead vampires will be added and artists will retouch the action to the demise and ignominy of vampires as originally intended!

Ram – You said you were given final approval rights for the script. That should count for something, Vlad. Why don't you call on your producer friend, Spielberg?

Vlad – I've learned that the original producers backed out when they learned of my intentions for the film and the new producer declined to offer the same arrangement. But at least we were able to force their hand... And it seems their major concern is money and what, lives? (says sarcastically) They're still willing to go ahead with printing and distribution... (motioning to Renfield) Renfield, it is time. (Renfield snaps on the T.V.)

Sue - (news anchorwoman) Tonight on Hot Topics we spotlight important movie news. Our guest is Vlad Dracula who has a second movie in the works. He has anxiously persuaded us, no doubt using famous hypnotic powers, to let our viewers hear what he thinks about life and well, death. Hello Vlad!

Vlad - Good Evening.

Sue - Our first caller has a question...

Caller - Like... if you become a vampire, does that mean you lose your soul? Or does that only happen when you die for real, like hundreds of years later? God forbid, uh excuse me. (coughs)

Vlad - If you refuse to receive undying life then you give up. For those of you who are religious, and receive the gift you will have a soul in the truest sense for what is more soulful than to exist and want to live? It is only the desire and will to live that can be attributed to the soul. It's what has existed from the very beginnings of life itself, it's very definition you might say. Without that you are merely dead... and what you've done waits to decay around your grave. (He waves the camera away. The screen shows shocked news people reacting.)

Caller - Uh thanks, I guess that covers it...

Rick - (newsman) Now that's charisma if I've ever heard it folks. I buy it! (laughs nervously) But wait a minute (gets an idea), vampires usually don't give you a choice in these things and you're talking about neck biting, aren't you?

Dirk - (newsman) Maybe he's giving us a choice now so he can lure enough of his people into that army of his... Vampires! (looks sideways to Dracula, who sneers) So then... later we won't have a choice. Anybody left will be feasted on by hordes of the hateful creatures. (He smiles at Vlad.)

Rick - My advice to viewers, caution maybe the watchword here! Now let's hear from Dracula's co-star in Bubble Bath of Blood, Brazen Gillpuppy live via remote hookup...

Brazen - All I can say is that if you have to... then go see his movie but he really is evil in every way. (shaking her head) Of course it's hard to retain your *purity or sanity* working in Hollywood. (She smiles sweetly.) But Vlad had only been here a few short weeks when he... Anyway (waves the camera away) if he wins the Oscar don't forget he debuted with me!

Sue - (to Vlad) What I don't understand is if you're talking about the movie or real life? (she looks somewhat embarrassed) I mean you're not suggesting that vampires are real? (Vlad stares at her apparently willing her to change the subject, she looks away.)

Rick - I didn't say that, did you? (looks at Dirk sheepishly)

Dirk - Me, neither. (adds quickly) No further questions Vlad!

Rick - (talking fast) The movie will be attacking Vlad's fans at your local cinema. Don't miss it! (Camera on Sue looking frustrated, then back to the monitor of Brazen Gillpuppy with a bored expression before cutting to commercial.)

Cyrule - Not a bad Countess, Vlad. Now we see the true reason for breaking tradition... a failed attempt at an actress? Pretty though, might even be worth the trouble.

Vlad - Go ahead, mince garlic. Of course she did have her chance and may yet have another. You would understand if you'd seen the movie.

Osiris - Sure Vlad, it happens. Say after our movie hits, they'll be screaming for our fangs. Maybe before! Just wait... That will put your first movie in a better light. It'll probably triple his fans, eh Renfield?

Renfield - I suppose if they came at night... We have many rooms. I could lock them in. Would you like that master?

Vlad - No, well maybe a few. I much prefer brief encounters at local cemeteries or bars, or on rare occasions Renfield brings something for me... Now I suppose we'll have a measure of added security, being with such old friends.

Ram - He calls us old. I seem to recall that you refused the carbon 14 test dating on a bet. (Vlad gazes at the ceiling.) Not to say we don't already know who among us predates the fossils of the earliest recognizable hominids, perhaps the missing link itself? (he laughs) Wasn't it the Neanderthal race who paid the price of your early existence? (laughing again) Perhaps it's irrelevant really which of us must assume a more modern appearance so as not to be sold to a circus, or some zoological research lab... the local dog pound? (Vlad shrugs after considering the pale countenance but smooth complexion of the smirking Ram.)

Vlad - It's fairly easy to see who wants to be the circus clown. I just wish Armageddon were here, he always loved to fight you. Remember how you used to incinerate yourselves with your antics, just like children. Now he's gone, gone off with aliens? I can't believe it...

One - Yes into the final void of nothingness, such an empty fate... The rumors say there were witnesses though.

Osiris - It's possible. God knows there's something out there, and buggery experts too from what I've heard.

Vlad - (scratching his head) With Armageddon here, I know it would be no contest to win the majority of humans. His theatrics were unsurpassed. The ancient theologians would have been amazed to realize they were describing a vampire when they wrote their fiery book of Revelations! Just to see the looks on their faces if they could know that there is one entity, a gifted vampire, who so closely embodies the forces described in their writings... chosen to end the world itself if necessary, Armageddon!

One - Amen.

Ram - I don't know, maybe people should try being machines awhile first! Maybe we all should... (The others smile at Vlad and then frown at Ram. Vlad is expressionless and continues to look out a window... At that moment a shooting star streaks silently through the Earth's outer atmosphere dissipating heat as it traverses the horizon, and appears to strike the ground with incredible velocity somewhere at a moderate distance in the adjoining hills. Vlad shakes his head at the coincidence, looking to the heavens. The others don't seem to notice.)

Ram - Now we've done the 'star thing,' and paid our dues. Let's have some fun with celebrity! I bet it'll be pretty strange now after such pervasive publicity to be under the neon lights of downtown Hollyweird, eh Vlad?

One - Maybe the less popular spots first...

Osiris - I doubt we'll be overnight sensations, especially considering Vlad's movie friends. They're probably planning another movie to kill off our characters as we speak.

Cyrule - Maybe they'll want to come after us and kill us in person, a simple blood hunt! I could go for a bite to eat!

One - Alright, it's settled, some fast food on Hollywood Boulevard. You coming Vlad?

Vlad - Tomorrow maybe, but enjoy... I'll see you then. (He retires to his coffin.)

PART V

ARMAGEDDON

The next evening finds Dracula watching the nightly news.

Sue - Tonight's topic is of course the sudden meteoric crash that occurred in Hollywood Hills late last night awakening the scientific community to explore the baffling origins of the event, which may possibly be remnants of a small comet. An alien crash has not been ruled out yet either. The celestial event and recent exotic weather disturbances in the area have also sparked debate in religious circles concerning ramifications surrounding the year 2020 A.D. and conjecture about the possibility for the second coming of Jesus Christ, albeit some twenty years off the mark... by most estimates.

John - Yes Sue and for such a large meteor to strike the earth without warning is unusual. (coughs) As we all know this comes somewhat near the two thousandth birthday anniversary of the acknowledged Son of God. As your co-anchor bringing you the very best in up-to-the-minute news, let me say that I'm glad to be on the story. (smiles at Sue) As Sue mentioned, it's thought that recent events may herald the Biblical prophecy hidden within the book of Revelations! (says with emotion and obvious discomfort.)

1

The screen then cuts to action cam shots of news crews at the burned out crater. Narration continues...

John - While scholars differ greatly in their interpretations of the Bible, the book of Revelations, and expectations revolving around the second or first (says under his breath), coming of a God entity, leader, savior, redeemer what have you... Well expectations have culminated into a fervor among religious communities that might be compared to the feelings children experience during the twelve days preceding Christmas. After all the Roman calendar has been adopted worldwide and has been faithfully marking time since before Jesus, including leap years. It has been argued though that the creator, being more or less a lover of chaos and natural selection, might have little use for milestones of ordered time... Still recent occurrences bear watching and this previously uncharted comet or very large meteor will be a closely followed story.

Rick - In an unrelated story, traffic was tied up for several hours along

The Reemergence of Vlad!

Hollywood Boulevard last night as men dressed as cyberspace vampires from the popular video game paraded, attracting hordes of fanatics and young devotees to vampirism similarly garbed in black. Whether the spectacle was staged or just an unusual reaction of denizens who frequent the late night clubs upon seeing their video idols in costume... is not known. The ensemble resembled a macabre funeral procession and may be in part publicity for a new movie as it was later confirmed that the berobed leaders are also the co-stars of Vlad Dracula. 'Dracula, The Reemergence of Vlad' has recently finished filming and is slated for quick release. (The screen shows images of the periphery of the crowd as it moves down the street and how people are at first upset at the obstruction then seem to join in willingly.) Vlad was apparently absent and there were no reported injuries but a few bystanders remarked that many of the cult-like cadre were openly bleeding from neck wounds... or so they would have us believe! The realism these days of advertisers knows no bounds... Wouldn't you agree Sue?

Sue - I'll pass on this one. I'm still recovering from the open forum we had with Vlad and his candid opinions about the human soul.

John - His confidence is remarkable isn't it, almost as if he's all-knowing or has some inside track on the subject! (Sue looks puzzled and upset. John continues in her place.) Now (cough) on to weather!

2

Dracula snaps off the T.V., musing to himself.

Vlad - Interesting. No wonder they haven't returned, letting themselves get caught up in a frenzy of publicity... The timing is appropriate. (There is a loud knock at the front door. Renfield comes from the kitchen and they both look to see seams of bright phosphorescent light seeping through around the front door. Dracula nods with expressive eyes to Renfield. Renfield opens the door.)

Armageddon - (entering while Renfield retreats behind the door... His entire body appears to be glowing a milky white even through light absorbent black clothes.) Had the damnedest time finding the place, Vlad... Only the faintest trail remains of your signal. Maybe the smog got it! (He laughs, and Dracula laughs as well seeing his old friend.)

Vlad - Renfield come out of there!

3

Renfield begins to emerge from hiding but notices the presence of a half a dozen diminutive alien beings gathered at the doorway and retreats behind the door's protection. The aliens appear as they are typically portrayed... slender, with somewhat elongated limbs, proportionately larger heads, large black eyes and emanating a milky white fluorescence from their skin or covering. Arm beckons them further.

Vlad - Well come on in, you'll probably attract less attention in here. (He gestures a greeting to Arm's guests.) I should have guessed you'd been up to something and that the reports, as they say, of your death were exaggerated! (They go to embrace but as Vlad's protruding incisors inch toward his companion's neck, Vlad is stopped.)

Arm - Hold up a minute! Same old Vlad, rather taste my blood as a dog might sniff another than believe anything I say.

Vlad - I'm sorry, it's the excitement. I've just completed a movie (he looks for signs that Arm understands the word) and you do look somewhat strange... forgive me. Tell your friends to make themselves at home. Renfield! (He scurries to the kitchen like a cockroach avoiding a predator.)

Arm - (motions to the aliens who affix themselves two to a chair in a relaxed profound silence) I'm still a vampire, if that's what worries you. And these are emissaries of goodwill or that is how they'd like to be portrayed to the media, anyway.

Vlad - (interrupting) Have you really just come from out there? (His eyes indicate the heavens as if examining the roofs of their sockets.)

Arm - Yes of course. I'd been actively searching for aliens for some time before actually. I'd heard some stories, you know, like the ones you'd hear in the old country centuries ago about vampires. You seldom hear stories anymore, it's all T.V. or books. Before, just the way locals would talk made your blood curdle, or theirs rather. Anyway I knew these tales I'd heard must be true. They were only passed by word of mouth and told with such emotion... and best of all, there were living witnesses. So I was hooked and followed the most recent patterns until I found them myself, in England. They were elusive as you might expect and seemed to enjoy playing on the image of leprechauns, magical elves of the forest. (Aliens appear more at ease enjoying the story, even playful.) But they usually don't make it a habit to spend much time away from their crafts. The ships can bend polarized light so well as to be invisible, even when nearing starlight. They don't so much fear provoking a panic or hostility as the problems they might create on their own. There have been landing mishaps and casualties before, especially in the Midwest U.S. Last night's landing was a little rough as well. (The aliens are now more serious.)

Vlad - Yes, there have been some attempted documentaries, even a lost alien autopsy film rediscovered in the nineties, fifty years after that mishap... Roswell, right? (The aliens wince and react uncomfortably.)

Arm - That was a major event, craft and crew destroyed. There have been others also due to too many crafts at similar altitudes and being undetectable as they are... sometimes to each other. They're also sensitive about their bodies. So they still rarely allow themselves to be seen. (The aliens nod slightly in affirmation.) Now that you know what I've been up to, where are the other troublemakers... placing some new blight on mankind? Or have they left already?

Vlad - Have you lived on another world as well?

Arm - No, not really... just on their ships but they are similar enough to home. They keep them stationed up there hovering, sanctuaries in space that are unfortunately close enough to damage the ozone. (He gives the aliens a condescending glance.) As you can imagine it takes enormous amounts of time to travel space, so they just stay. (Vlad nods.) So what's this about then? (He asks as if Vlad has interrupted a family meal.)

Vlad - (appearing dazed, ignoring the aliens) Well they said they wouldn't be gorging but I just saw them on T.V., a news report, blocking traffic in an obvious orgy of blood lust... not able to content themselves with being stars in my new movie... and now like animals openly parading in the streets, upstaging everything of course.

Arm - You don't say? Maybe they've been drugged. Biting young people in these times, you never know what you'll find coursing in their blood. If the old crones have started a blood frenzy, that kind of feeding could lead to all sorts of lethal drug combinations... if they were human! (laughs)

Vlad - Or even in young vampires, exactly! There's already a small army of new vampires. I started about a hundred myself just before they arrived... already too many to properly instruct. The movie may provide guidance. All they know at this point is how to propagate.

Arm - Inner city vampires, I know the type...

Vlad - Yes, many mere children and not aware that there are other reasons for the gift.

Arm - I wasn't aware myself and will reserve judgment on that point until (squints eyes and concentrates) you tell me (trying to perceive Dracula's thoughts) or until the final conflagration! Which ever comes first. (Dracula's brow furrows from either concentration or surprise.) You know, the be all and end all event to culminate humanity, cap it off so to speak... (Vlad eye's widen with raised brows.) You don't think it's here so soon? (Dracula nods, looking relieved.) The Bible... with prophets, witnesses, the book of Revelations, my namesake for heaven sake? The way, the truth, the light? For God sakes say something Vlad!

Vlad - You know I don't care about such things, even abhor them....

Arm - If Armageddon were here, we'd know it. (smiles) Personally, I think it's a ways off, there are none of the basic signs... angels, that sort of thing. (speaking quickly)

Vlad - But Armageddon may already be here in a different guise... artificial immortality. (Arm nods sagely, immune to insult.) Another name is Cyborg from the science of cybernetics, the melding of human identity into mechanical form! (As Vlad talks the aliens become animated, gesturing and making high-pitched synthesized sounds, somewhat like the mother ship in 'Close Encounters.') Do they understand?

Arm - Oh yes. Though they sound it, they're not robotic themselves. (Just then Renfield enters with a tray of blood filled glasses, setting them before the guests.) Good man Renfield! (He says while coughing. Renfield smiles fawningly and departs.)

Vlad - They drink?

Arm - They can assimilate about anything given enough time... (Renfield disappears into the kitchen.)

Vlad - Anyway here is the proof. I've shown the others as well. (He spreads out dozens of clipped newspaper articles on the table that deal with recent scientific advances in cybernetics: technical discussions, ethical considerations, current progress in prototypes, etc. An article on top is titled, Mind Transplant or Human Head on Robot Body?

Arm - No idle threat I see. But still, vampires have always been what we are, the scourge of humanity, the bane of all existence. How will humans, arising with an alternate form of immortality change things? And will bringing us out in the open after long centuries serve to stir up jealousy and hatred, and make us despised and hunted once more? They'll never accept us for what we are! Of course people may say that we're lawless, vile spreaders of disease and death. Still, at the root of their prejudice is jealousy. But then you know! How can you forget Transylvania, your impregnable castle, vampires running in wolf packs through the countryside scaring everybody out of their minds? It didn't last. The peasants banded together with their garlic and crosses.

Vlad – Of course I remember.

Arm - Yes. Well then you know the damage tourists can do and the nightmare endured by the vampires that chose to remain. I doubt there's one within five hundred miles of the castle today. (Renfield carries in another tray, this one containing an arrangement of cockroaches with wooden splinters as toothpicks thrust through their middles. He also has a bowl and crackers.)

Renfield - Excuse me master. I think our guests are still hungry. (He glances at the aliens with fascination.) I have some termite pudding and saltines and a nice assortment of...

Vlad - Please Renfield. No termites... I need some air. (Renfield removes the pudding but leaves the other fare. Dracula gets up and walks around. The aliens consider the platter and the cockroaches, some of which are alive though skewered, and sample them nonchalantly.) Armageddon... the symbolic ending of the world. Arm our world is ending! What are we to do, give up? 'Lie in our coffins for a thousand years? (He switches on a transistor radio... They sit in the dark listening.)

Radio Reporter - This is Brad and you're on WYMI with a special satellite broadcast, the midnight follow-up report of the strange doings down on Main Street, also known as Hollywood Boulevard, earlier tonight... Traffic was at a standstill as actors dressed as vampires from the movie 'Dracula, The Reemergence of Vlad' and a huge entourage progressed both east and west, or as one witness put it, 'this way and that,' passing popular nightspots along the way and swelling their ranks. People were even observed abandoning cars to proceed with the group to its undetermined destination in Hollywood Hills. We're talking Mercedes, Lexus's and Jags folks... in the streets for the taking! More on the story as it becomes available... One further note though is that there have been no arrests yet, and that the 'vampires' will likely not be charged with blocking traffic... for the simple reason that traffic is always blocked at that time of night as any serious frequenter of the area knows. The city would be leaving itself open to lawsuits from a rash of unwarranted arrests, something to be avoided and all too familiar in Hollywood, a town as we all know with no short supply of hot tempered litigious movie stars!

Vlad – (to Arm) They may be drunk but they're attempting to further the cause, though perhaps prematurely. (They then begin to hear sounds of a massive gathering outside the house and neighboring wooded areas.) They may also be completely losing their senses!

4

Vlad opens the door to the throng and sees One, Osiris and Ram with lurid smiles. They are covered in blood and countless new vampires are sporting hungry teeth. Some are already in the form of bats, examining their large folding wings. Arm comes up alongside Vlad to watch and their radiant presence seems to interest the crowd. One motions to Vlad to say something...

One - Lord Dracula, Prince Vlad Tepes of Wallachia, born of the blood of Dracule the Dragon... your children await! At long last your blood is made one again! (The vampires show their eagerness with flapping wings and glance about like animals.)

Vlad - This is all new, very new to you now and soon you will be hungry. (Some eye the necks of others to be slapped back. Some take others unaware but release their biteholds quickly not able to enjoy drinking from other vampires.) But the gift of life is yours! Use it to your advantage and you will find new strength. (The vampires make vocal hissing noises and flapping sounds in support.) Now go, this is no religion! By organizing we identify ourselves to the enemy. Watch our movie and understand who would harm us! (Vlad turns his back and enters the house.)

One - Go my children or fly, those who may and return to the sacred earth. Master the darkness and remember the One who commands, whose blood that reigns! Dracula, the lord of night in all eternity! (With great commotion and flapping, the sky fills with winged creatures. Those not yet converted or unable to fly amble away in the darkness, some coughing... feeling the undersized wings sprouting from their backs. As the crowd disperses the aliens appear at the door and raise their arms in a belated greeting.)

5

The next day helicopters circle the area repeatedly at various intervals and leave, apparently unsatisfied. But news vans with camera crews are parked at the ready outside the house where the street ends. And at least one cameraman is constantly stationed near Dracula's front door with a portable shoulder camera. The huge lens peers through the small door window hoping to catch some sign of life from within. All that is noticed is the dark well-shaded gloom and the buzzing of a fly against the inner side of the windowpane... The scene cuts away to the inside of the house to show Renfield crouched listening against the other side of the door. He notices the fly. The scene shifts back again to the camera's lens waiting outside and seconds later the camera catches an eager tongue rushing up to smash fly against window, and Renfield's face also pressed squarely to the glass just inches in front of the camera's lens. Renfield stares back vacantly before devouring the insect... The startled cameraman leaps to his feet and flees leaving his camera behind. Renfield retreats further within the house as the sound of squealing tires and straining engine reaches him then fades away.

Later in the afternoon several police LAPD cruisers and a dark blue car with FBI in large white letters on the side and hood pull up to join the remaining news van still waiting at the cul-de-sac.

Detective Demater - (in a perfunctory manner) We got the search warrant, wouldn't want a technicality to get in in the way of this one. (to newsmen) C'mon boys if you're game! (The cameramen pick up cameras and follow...) Let's see that picture again. (Another detective takes out a Polaroid showing dozens of blurry dark webbed figures near the front of the house, the front door open and imposing caped visages just outside. They reach the front door.) Just as I suspected, the old non-existent address ploy... (He points to an area showing where the house's address numbers had been recently removed. He knocks loudly and shouts.) We've got a warr... ant. (Renfield has already opened the door before he can finish the word. Renfield looks almost presentable in his long coat and combed hair but some large ant-like insects are noticeably crawling on his head and shoulders.)

Renfield - Please come in officers, it's alright you're expected. (He holds out his hand. Demater walks past but the second detective, surprised gives it a hasty shake. His facial expression does little to conceal a strange feeling of uneasiness.) You're welcome to see whatever you'd like, perhaps the kitchen first? (smiling overanxiously) And something to eat... (Detective Demater turns back to Renfield.)

Demater - Listen Mr.

Renfield - Yes, the master is not here, I am the Mister... I like that!

Demater - Whoever you are, you're in trouble. We have to cuff you and after we've searched, you're going downtown. (He motions to the other detective to cuff Renfield.)

2nd Detective - (looks at Renfield queerly) What've you got on you, and on your hands? (Renfield reveals a hand filled with termites.)

Renfield - In the kitchen, a snack...

2nd Detective - (shudders then notices the mush of termites on his own hand) Ughhh.

Renfield - A towel...? 'Just a moment. (He opens a nearby door in the hall. As he enters the detective grabs the back of his coat.)

2nd Detective - Hey where do you think... (He realizes he is now in possession of Renfield's coat, but Renfield is not in it. He drops it immediately to avoid the bugs. On opening the door further there is no sign of Renfield.) He's gone!

Demater - What?

2nd Detective - 'Just a small closet and his coat (pushes on the wall to no avail) but no mister! (says with a laugh) Just as well. (He hangs up the coat gingerly.)

Demater - What!?

The Reemergence of Vlad!

2nd Detective - 'Full of bugs... (starts shivering and grimacing) Let's get this over with! (The cameraman nods in agreement and films the empty closet.)

FBI man - (leading the way) This looks like the kitchen... (The second detective stops short.)

2nd Detective - I'll pass. (He opens another nearby door off the main hallway instead, descending the stairs carefully with a flashlight. The stairs are steep and he notices a repaired step near the top. He becomes more and more queasy as he reaches the last step, and has to hold the wall for support. He shines his light over the ground and sees freshly dug earth but nothing else. He returns to the main floor and waits... The others return from their investigations upstairs.

Demater - Nothing, no sign of anything except dust... And except for the main table which was recently used.

FBI man - There was some blood in the refrigerator...

Demater - Oh?

FBI man - Yea, we'll run some tests. There were plenty of glasses on hand but hardly any plates or serving ware... clean though.

Demater - I see. What about pots and pans?

FBI man - Plenty of them, or enough for a good sized gathering anyway.

Demater - Very good. (scratches head)

FBI man - 'Different style though...

Demater - What?

FBI man - Well the pots and pans were of a different style than the plates and serving ware... the later from a more economical set of cutlery. 'May not be important.

Demater - You may be right. There wasn't much upstairs either. Most of the rooms are locked. Do your electronics pick up anything?

FBI man - Nothing human... some infrared readings that may be insect colonies, possibly rodents. Of course I can't pick up dead bodies.

Demater - No, I understand. (smirks at second Detective - Ted) What's in the basement Ted, anything?

Ted - Nothing, just a lot of freshly turned earth...

Demater - What!?

Ted - And... when I was down there... there was something else.

Demater - What?

Ted - Well... something strange, unnatural you know, but I feel a little better now. (Demater shakes his head.)

FBI man - Give me a minute. (He descends the basement stairs and comes back up quickly, looking at his machine.) No, nothing. I wonder where our host could have gone?

Ted - They're supposed to be in the ground during the day. (The others look at him...) Vampires! If that's where they are, they seem authentic enough. You saw the picture... vampires! (They stop looking at him. The FBI man nods. Demater shakes his head. The cameraman starts filming Ted and gets a strong Italian gesture...)

FBI man - It might be possible they could be hiding in a near dormant state, if they can induce a state of shock, maybe with strong tranquilizers? Did you know possums can self-induce a state of paralytic shock, convincing as roadkill with rigor mortis!

The Reemergence of Vlad!

Demater - What!? I've had enough. I'm not paid enough for this. Forensics can come check it out. Let's go. (They file out of the house and as they drive away several aliens make an appearance at the doorway... then return inside and close the door.)

6

The scene has Vlad seated at a quiet bar with a modest number of clientèle. Most are watching an important news update following in the wake of the recent disturbances in Hollywood.

Rick (newsman) - Dear viewers, we've been through riots in Los Angeles, fires in the hills and earthquakes bringing destruction to Hollywood's doorstep. Even so, few would disagree that the unusual occurrences of the past week have wreaked more havoc in entertainment land. From Burbank to Malibu folks have been reeling as if feeling the effects of adrenaline jolted straight through the heart of central Hollywood!

Sue - Yes Rick, first an unprecedented weather formation reaching to the upper atmosphere, encircling the earth and pinpointing almost exactly a home in North Hollywood Hills... then a meteoric crash of a stony object which was later revealed to be a kind of disposable landing craft, disposable in the sense that it's unlikely it could have flown in any direction but down, and of a design alien to anything yet known by top military experts. In addition, subsequent crop patterns have been reported from the few corn fields in the LA vicinity as well as several actual alien sightings... though still unconfirmed. The sudden crop formations may only be the work of quirky farmers or migrant workers playing for attention at this sensitive time... of course.

Rick – Rural humor knows no bounds does it Sue?

Sue - Anyway, the day following the arrival of visitors from the heavens hordes of fanatics representing vampires, magicians or drug influenced impressionable youths engaged en masse in sadomasochistic rituals of consensual self mutilations. (pan to Rick grimacing) Most were bleeding from the neck as they rampaged through town finally converging at the house alluded to earlier by the account of strange weather. Police found nothing at the residence.

Rick - (regaining composure) That's right Sue...

Sue - (cutting him off) All this sounds too fantastic and may be just the beginning! Vampires have been known to embody powers of consummate evil and this one in particular, Vlad Dracula, has historically resorted to impaling victims on huge stakes... a mad charade of one of his own truly vulnerable weaknesses, that of an implement of wood hammered into his beastly heart!

John – Thank you Sue. (She is staring fixedly ahead, breathing fast and sweating.) That's quite enough. 'Seems you've gotten over your squeamishness. (regards her strangely) Well to offset the scores of missing or suspicious persons reported stalking areas around local graveyards, yesterday we were treated to a vision so majestic and awe-inspiring it could only be described as having Biblical implications, as an avowed miracle! Here's the footage, see for yourselves... (A tape is run showing Arm walking on the surface of the ocean near Santa Monica pier, wearing his black cape but glowing with a luminescence making even the clothes underneath the cape appear white with glowing light. Above him some twenty yards fly many large vampires displaying incredible leather wings flapping effortlessly amidst the background of a violent storm forming out at sea. The shot was taken by a news helicopter at dusk and the newsman's audible exclamations can be heard above the rumbles of thunder and thudding whirl of blades.)

Cameraman - Well it can't be a movie stunt, we're the only ones filming!

Pilot - Look, wherever he walks the water is calm, like... you know, the story in the Bible!

Cameraman - I see it...

7

A stranger at the bar next to Vlad nudges him and says, 'Maybe it's Armageddon!' and laughs. Vlad regards him with piercing eyes then turns back to the screen and nods slowly.

Rick - The vision reportedly vanished moments later enveloped by mist of the ensuing storm. And it has now been witnessed by millions and as you've seen was not a movie effect but a real event captured by newsmen, our newsmen at FAUX to be specific. (Behind them office phones start ringing off the hook.) We at FAUX have naturally anticipated a strong viewer reaction. (The camera switches to busy news secretaries attending phones and then back to Rick who is caught motioning to them to keep the noise level down.)

Sue - (interrupting)   May I?   Well, we would now like to introduce a prominent theologian in residence and professor at USC, known in past years for bringing the 'Us College' as it is affectionately known worldwide prominence in the area of Bible Studies (looks embarrassed) and religion, Jewish and otherwise I'd imagine... Professor Israel.

Professor Israel - (looking sage and speaking with an accent)   What we've just seen I am convinced represents no less than an act of God, a miracle in modern times, a manifestation of the Holy Spirit, a form of divinity, possibly the Christ himself on earth.   This is the third of a group of major heavenly signs which Biblical scholars from around the world, my colleagues in theology *believe* (emphasizes the word) may indeed herald the apocalypse!

John - Yes, of course that's most interesting and would that mean that there will indeed be a second coming of Jesus the Christ? If what we've just seen can be substantiated as real...   And is there any solid basis in the scriptures to support this idea?

Professor Israel - (nodding solemnly) We believe there is. The vexing question now really is why Israel herself was not the preferred setting for such an event. But then who can pretend to know the mind of God?

John - I plead not guilty on that count! (The other newscasters cough, shake their heads.)   But let's not sidestep the question our viewers want answered. Any possible confirmation for such a fantastic conclusion?

Professor Israel - As most of us who have read the Bible know, the scriptures offer a variety of interpretations in reference to the final judgment. What we've witnessed is a storm opening to the heavens, ominous dark angels above and an apparition of divinity wearing a black robe...   These things may not portend well for the final outcome sad to say.

Sue - In view of the reports of scores of vampires or vampire-like people seen on Hollywood Boulevard, and their similarity in appearance to the dark angels... Could you comment on that?

Professor Israel - Well I know of no specific mention of vampires in the Bible but the symbolism in the book of Revelations suggests that there may be dragons or other beasts with wings. And these could have prophetic implications for vampires or similar creatures... (rubbing his chin)

Sue - (turning to the front camera) Well you heard it on FAUX first! Renowned scholars are playing this fast and loose, predicting that a recent rapid succession of unexplained unnatural incidents may mean an apocalypse... Armageddon if you will and any major cataclysmic ending, religious or otherwise, would no doubt come too soon for most of us. How much time do we have, would you say months? (looks at Professor, who doesn't respond) Sooner? (He shrugs his shoulders and nods an affirmation.) That is disturbing! Our own research department here at FAUX have been doing a little Bible study of its own and here is John with the relevant findings from the Book of Revelations!

John – Thank you Sue. As most of us know Revelations is often overlooked by serious theologians due to its inscrutable character. The writing has never been clearly understood... and is cryptic at best. (The camera cuts quickly to the professor then back.) The purpose of the author appears to be that of enigma and confusion. There has been little hope of further clues until now. Numerology within the text may provide a key or code to help unlock hidden predictions... The number forty two in this instance may have added significance for us today. I quote, 'The holy city is trampled for forty two months by other nations.' This may be a reference to Jerusalem, long considered a holy city and capital of Israel... or in a larger context a reference to Israel which historically has been in constant conflict with other nations since early recorded history. In this larger context the four might represent four thousand years prior to Christ and the two, the two thousand years since. By interesting coincidence Bible scholars deciphering lineages recorded in the book of Genesis have determined the year four thousand and four B.C. to be the year God created man. With that in mind we can then subtract the extra four years from the more obvious target date of two thousand and thirty three A.D., the two thousandth anniversary of Jesus' death and arrive at the present year, 2029 A.D. for our projected date of annihilation. Fortunately, for those of us who may require more reassurance, historians have determined that the ancient calender may be off by as many as thirty years though they're not sure which direction, which would make it sixty years in all wouldn't it?

For those of you who may be interested, Revelations contains many other numbers also without apparent importance until now... They are, in order: 4, 7, 10, 12, 24, 144, 666, 1000, and 1260. The number seven is mentioned most prominently of all and is used to describe angels, seals, scrolls, churches, plagues, variously colored horses... (loud coughing from Professor Israel)

Professor Israel - (interrupting) I wonder if before I leave I might be allowed to quote a verse from the living word? (He begins reading aware there is little time before they cut to commercial.) Revelations I verse 3, 'Blessed is he who reads aloud the words of prophecy, and he who hears, etc. etc.,' (then louder) 'for the time is near!' (He crosses himself and prays silently...)

The Reemergence of Vlad!

8

Still at the bar, Dracula is drumming his heavily nailed fingers on the polished surface of the wood. The sound is something like a woodpecker. He listens while the T.V. news anchor now speaks of a strange plague condition afflicting the cast, crew and extras from the set of a locally filmed science fiction movie. As many as two hundred people have been affected but their names and which movie is being kept confidential due to the undetermined nature of the illness and security reasons. The newsmen joke that the movie producers will probably release the information as soon as they realize the publicity will help sell the film... 'Besides,' Rick argues, 'Vampirism isn't the sort of thing that should be kept hidden, but thrust into the light of day!' They laugh.

Fanatic - (a religious fanatic at the bar suddenly loses control of himself and starts proclaiming...) You're all sinners and the heavy hand of God will smite you down! Save yourselves while there's still time!

Bartender - (yelling) Hey no solicitors, move along. (He escorts the fanatic outside.)

Guy Next to Dracula - (talking in Vlad's direction) A real miracle! Then they talk about some kooky movie... Hey, I guess life goes on. (laughs) Mister do you realize that sort of thing hasn't happened in two thousand years? And we're here to see it! Can you beat that? (Vlad makes an effort to grin at the man then turns back to the television. Siskel and Ebert are next reviewing 'a hot new movie about cold dead things... cybernetic robots versus vampires! Stay tuned.' After a commercial break...)

Siskel - The movie seems to be lacking in every category including some new categories that could only exist with this particular film... However there is something endearing in the vampire's adherence to their cause and in the ways they engage their enemies, the futuristic cyborgs. Though by rights the vampires should be hopelessly out gunned, there is a surprise ending. One other thing that grabbed me I have to admit is the realism. They had to have gone through quite a few stunt men and dedicated extras to get that extent or degree of injury that comes across on screen...

Ebert - I don't know Gene, a lot of that action was probably shot with real cyborgs as test dummies. If so, this film has just pushed the boundaries of live computer animatronic action. Special effects are fun but after the hundredth movie, one starts to wonder where the thrill has gone. A curious footnote with 'Reemergence' that I'm compelled to mention is the sizable grassroots following generated before its general release. Apparently the one or two preview screenings in L.A. were enough to strike a chord with a fanatic following... as if they'd been lying dormant in their coffins waiting for the reappearance of a masterful vampire capable of leadership. This particular Dracula possesses a concerned almost human side as well and is a welcome addition to the trademark ruling Count of Transylvania attitude we tend to see from the movie industry. So see it if you have to and make it a matinée preferably. To those from the LA area who haven't seen it yet you may want to plan to stay home at night at least if you live in Hollywood!

Siskel - Right Roger, very similar to the 'Rocky Horror' situation in New

York but worse. Curious is certainly the word for it. I did some checking and regretfully there are no more prerelease showings scheduled in L.A.!

Ebert – That's strange, only a limited showing of our new Dracula's preview then... (He shrugs. A picture of Vlad with cape covering his face below the eyes is flashed on the screen.) I'm afraid we don't have much of a trailer either. Oh well. 'Could be there are some post production snags stemming from what they're now referring to as the LA Creature Feature riots that have been creating havoc along Hollywood Boulevard at night these days... Don't worry we'll keep all you loyal vampire fans posted!

9

Vlad unconsciously takes a sip from an untouched beer that has been in front of him and grimaces, then wipes the foam away with his cape. The man sitting next to him notices his identity but Vlad stares with hypnotic piercing eyes...

Guy Next to Dracula - Those things give me the creeps, just one step up from 'Friday the Thirteenth' if you ask me... I'm a western man myself. (smiles) Of course I've seen all the Sharon Stone movies but when it comes to a male dominated flick... you know real machismo with guns and guys bleeding from the mouth, you can't beat a western!

Vlad - (eyes the man suavely then talking to himself...) Not a bad review considering what's been said of vampires before.

Guy at Bar - Say you're one of these movie people aren't you? You probably have something to do with that new gorge they're throwing up on the screen I bet. You ought to be ashamed, maybe even punished or something... What kid wants to watch some fancy pants vampire, can't tell if he's man or woman... hiding his face behind drapery, what kind of hero is that? Huh? (Vlad has already departed the bar.)

10

He flies in search of another bar that might contain his companions... He notices a popular club on Sunset Boulevard painted black with glow in the dark stars and the name, 'Night Walkers.' There are several couples outside with heads buried in each other's necks, much too energetic for normal necking. One looks up as Vlad walks by exposing the small open wound of his victim to the night air. Vlad enters... Inside he finds Arm who is no longer glowing and the others seated at a table near the back, away from the action at the floor.)

Vlad - (clasps Arm on the shoulder as he sits...) Arm! A cunning stunt, a giant among vampires... I knew you'd surpass even your own abilities!

Arm - And now your movie will manage to have a huge following even without me in a starring role! But you have these two to thank for the fact there may soon be more vampires than humans walking the streets. (Ram and One raise a toast. Vlad notices the glasses contain blood.)

Vlad - Where? (He regards their glasses questioningly. They indicate an area next to the wall where several young girls are passed out lying against each other and sporting fresh neck wounds.)

One - A going away party then? We don't want to wear out a welcome. They'll be coming with hammers and stakes, or worse! You know the minds of desperate widows, orphans, abandoned husbands and mistresses, and the like... They never change.

Vlad - What of your other world friends, Arm? Are they able to be left on their own?

Arm - Don't worry, Renfield said he was going to the movies and wanted to bring them along! (They enjoy the joke...)

11

Meanwhile... the scene switches to a large multiplex cinema. Police cars are scattered all around the area, lights flashing. The aliens are huddled in a group in the middle of the theater lobby, and are wearing oversized clothes and hats. Renfield is off to the side trying to look inconspicuous and blend in with other movie patrons. About twenty officers using the fancy theater barriers have cordoned off the area around the diminutive, mildly glowing beings. Two supervisory officers are explaining the situation to Detective Demater.)

Demater - Happened to be near, tracking some crazed terrorist would be vampires. And naturally suddenly everyone's a fanatic about vampires!

1st Supervisor Officer - You're not after the 'Vampire of Armageddon?'

That's what they're calling him, you know the one on the news yesterday. A lot of people think he might be... supernatural. They're going to let the Pope decide.

Demater - I swear we'll have half the town behind bars if we start bringing in these weirdos. Now it's aliens is it?

1st Supervisor Officer - Look for yourself they're right over there! (looking in the direction of the spectacle)

Demater - I know where they are, but for the sake of clarity, why are they there? Just once to humor me okay?

2nd Supervisor Officer - Why not, you're the boss... (Demater shakes his head.) It seems they had tickets or someone bought them for them. We suspect that strange looking guy... He's holding a bag of bugs, beetles I think. I checked. (The officer smiles, proud of his work of detection.)

Demater - (scrutinizing the aliens from a distance and noting the large black eyes and heads, elongated limbs, glowing skin) Tickets! Tickets? They had tickets, go on...

2nd Supervisor Officer - Well, someone noticed them... a ticket girl, because it's night and they were glowing. I guess it was noticeable. See they're still glowing!

1st Supervisor Officer - Maybe they want to be brought you know, to a leader. They haven't said anything though. C'mon inspector, they're right over here... (motions for him to follow)

Demater - I'm the detective, and I think I'll pass. Get them to the station then if they're friendly or if they aren't. (They look eager to tackle their task.) You may want to exercise a little caution at first, until they start vaporizing us!

The Reemergence of Vlad!

(They stop in their tracks and squint their eyes with determination, then continue slowly. Demater approaches Renfield...) Do you (emphasizing the word) *speak* any English sir?

Renfield - Yes I was just minding my business officer. I mean there is no business, just the movies and...

Demater - Yes?

Renfield - They followed me.

Demater - And how long have they been following you?

Renfield - Just a few days.

Demater - What!?

Renfield - I mean I saw them before at the house, they crashed nearby. I was friendly, offered what food I had and then the next thing I knew they were following me here... the truth, I swear!

Demater - I don't suppose you had a phone to report something of this nature?

Renfield - No, I'm sorry officer, the master doesn't permit... (Detective Demater is distracted by the operation to herd the aliens out the lobby.)

Demater - Okay you but I want you to leave your name and address with... (As soon as Demater utters the word *leave* Renfield is making his way through the crowd and out into the night. Demater realizes Renfield's gone and discovers ants crawling on his coat. He mutters...) That's okay I think I know where to find you. (He holds an ant for closer inspection.)

(On the way home Renfield is approached by several young vampires. He smiles showing his craggy teeth and offers them beetles. They hiss and turn away, he hurries home.)

12

The next night Dracula and Renfield are at home watching the evening news on T.V.

Vlad - Well Renfield was there much trouble removing the sarcophagus for shipment back to Egypt?

Renfield - It was difficult master but I used the cellar window. It was picked up in the afternoon.

Dracula - I didn't know we had a cellar window?

Renfield - Yes master.

Dracula - The others had most of the fun. Osiris told me he spent a lot of time marveling at the tall buildings downtown, especially the architecture of Century City... probably looking for burial chambers. (The T.V. comes to life with the voice of the news announcer...)

Sue - This is Sue Orenthal of FAUX Broadcast Network Action Line News... The first irrefutable and instantly documented alien encounter may have occurred last night at one of Hollywood's cinemas. A band of four small glowing white skinned beings were taken into custody of police without incident and brought to Cedar Sinai Hospital for observation and tests. Medical scientists have determined that their physiology is radically different from humans. Their blood has high amounts of phosphorus which is found in laundry detergent and florescent lights and may explain their tendency to glow. There is a chance that they may hold the key to significant human medical advances. However a method of accurate communication has not been established, only drawings on paper, geometric designs that closely resemble crop formations reported from time to time in farmer's fields around the world and again more recently, and to a lesser extent city wall graffiti. (says haltingly) There have also been some unexplained sand structures being found on beaches. Could it be that these designs previously proven to be the work of ambitious hoaxers will once more become the focus of the world's top scientific minds? The jury's still out...

John - Yes Sue, and incredibly that story complete with its *little green glowing men* now takes precedence over the miraculous appearance of a manifestation, quite possibly divine in nature... I'm referring of course to the tall man with dark flowing robes seen walking upon the ocean waters with bat-like angelic creatures flying above him. This happened off the coast of Malibu, one of the world's most popular tourist stops. The Pope has still not ruled yet on whether this event will be chronicled an avowed miracle. Perhaps of even more immediate concern to the residents of Hollywood are the fantastic accounts of disappearances and blindingly quick attacks which have left victims anemic, shaken, dazed and forgetful... What I'm talking about here is the very real threat of vampirism or (reading quickly) the severely misguided fans who have somehow become fanatic enough to behave as *vampires* might if they did *exist!*

13

The scene switches to a bar T.V. in downtown Hollywood where all the patrons are apparently vampires.

John - (continuing) We here at FAUX are of the opinion that adequate precautions should be taken.

Rick - That's right John. There's no sense not knowing the proper way to fight these things... Say there's a two hundred pound punk breathing down your neck about to tap into your blood supply with teeth out to here... (motions with hands) If he believes he's an immortal vampire, do you think a cleverly concealed gun will be able to stop him? Well maybe, but what if it doesn't? (The bar erupts with loud hissing and the vampires cast about with vile stares. Someone comes up behind the news desk and whispers in Rick's ear. He reacts reflexively thinking he is about to be bitten then calms down and listens.) I've just been informed that if these creatures are real then announcing their weaknesses may give them advance warning and hinder efforts to subdue them. However I will say this... if you feel certain you've found one or one threatens your life then you should find a sharpened implement of wood and hammer. Now notice your chest, there is an area of central declivity, a shallow depression just below the breast bone or sternum. That's the spot, place the point of the stake in that unprotected zone and hammer away. Don't try for anything fancy between the ribs, you won't reach the heart and it will only anger the beast. (Rick wipes his forehead with a tissue. The vampires at the bar motion for the channel to be changed, and the bartender flips on the 'Tonight Show' with Jay Leno.)

14

The scene switches back to Dracula's house.

John - The scientific community would like to join FAUX in expressing the dangers of allowing a vampire's bite or engaging in vampire-like activity... Please try to remain calm and report any suspected alien or vampire sightings immediately to the local authorities. On a more positive note, we take solace in the fact that in light of these strange developments researchers across the country and the world have announced attempts to perfect the development of a cyborg man capable of encoding the exact personality patterns of individual human beings. The confirmed presence of alien and probability of vampire life forms has provided the final motivation and impetus according to a NASA spokesman to make the commitment to this new breakthrough in technological advancement. Hopefully what they have will be vastly superior to the alternatives we face... what is known of vampire existence or the maladaptive alien biology. We should pass along a message at this time to the hundreds of independent inventors who hold patents on similar ideas of cyborg technology for human longevity. The government has announced that its prototype is unique so you needn't bother trying to sue.

Sue - I guess it won't be long then as the monkey says... until we evolve into something else? (There's a brief pause while the other two newsmen look at her in embarrassed silence.)

John - It's interesting. (coughs) I talked with one of the researchers on the project. He said everyone has a peculiar thinking pattern which is usually formed in childhood and though it continually *evolves* can basically redevelop itself if recorded at an early stage. So even if we were to lose memories in this process we would still be very similar to our old selves eventually. Who needed those algebra classes anyway?

Rick - I didn't even like my childhood! (He laughs.)

Sue - But once we're machines we'll have time for new memories, is that it? (again, an embarrassed pause... she smiles at the camera.)

John - By the way if anyone has not yet had a chance to view Dracula's new movie, the one that's been sounding the alarm and pushing humanities' collective buttons so to speak... do so! In 'Vlad, The Reemergence' we see actual prototype cyborgs as actors defending against an eerily realistic maybe not so far-fetched threat of vampirism. The vampires are led by the new actor and veteran of two films now, of course Vlad Dracula, who else who may be an actual descendant of his historical namesake...

Sue - Say do you think he might really be a...?

John - No. (He laughs.)

Sue - Very interesting John, now on to Lloyd with our weather!

(At that moment the loud thumping sound of a low flying helicopter is heard overhead and Dracula snaps off the T.V.)

Pilot - Alright, we're over it now, anything with the infrared? Try the resonance imaging.

Copilot - There was something with red-heat... a small geometrical shape, a square, I think. Yea, like a T.V. maybe... It's fading now. Almost nothing.

Pilot - Check the settings.

Copilot - Yea, nothing else. Oh they forgot to upload the imager thingamajig. No here it is, angle closer to the windows for a better shot. (Renfield looks out to see the chopper almost on the roof.)

Pilot - Better not. Do you really think he's in there... you know, Jesus?

Copilot - No, I heard he caught the last train for the coast! Hey in that song, it was the east coast wasn't it?

Pilot - You're crazy, you know that?

Copilot - I'm up here with you, aren't I? Anyway you started it. Jesus' house! Then we're from the north pole with sacks of presents? (Their conversation fades out as they get further away...) Demater won't like this.

15

The last scene: Dracula and Renfield sit in silence somewhere in the dark.

Renfield - I think they've gone.

Dracula – Thank you Renfield.

Renfield - Master?

Dracula - Yes?

Renfield - If they come with their big weapons... We might do something. I will try my best, but if they do...

Dracula - Yes Renfield?

Renfield - I mean (crunching sounds) if they finally destroy you or just me... Could there be an afterworld for the completely dead?

Dracula - What is that sound? Are you eating?

Renfield - Sorry master.

Dracula - Even our nemesis the church sets its example for their children first, that they are in a sense what is an afterlife. Vampires may not have children in the usual way, nevertheless by now I would guess we have many thousands.

Renfield - I hope (crunching) we won't need them...

Dracula - Anyway, you needn't concern yourself, Renfield. What kind of parent would I be if I didn't look after my children?

Renfield - Master?

Dracula - Yes?

Renfield - Master? (hardly able to contain himself)

Dracula - What is it!

Renfield - (controlling himself then calmly) I'm worried about our friends from space. They haven't returned and they seemed to like it here. Do suppose they'll be alright?

Dracula - (speaking quickly) I wouldn't bother yourself on their account Renfield, at least not for their safety. Armageddon informed me that they are nearly a match for a vampire... in every sense supernatural, weighty opponents but fortunately slow to anger. And like the vampire tend not to stray long from home.

Renfield - I'm happy about that, maybe they are just trying to be popular (glances at Dracula) or like the young ones, your children and hiding as vampires must do... (with sudden realization) But maybe the wonderful things you've done will be blamed on them! (cocking his head in an act of submission)

Dracula - Yes Renfield, what are you saying?

Renfield - You wouldn't kill the aliens as you wanted with the Christians would you master?

Dracula - That might bring an Armageddon wouldn't it, if what Arm knows of their power is true. No, if we can exist with humans, Christians, women and the rest, I'm sure we can live with the small ones... for now.

Renfield - I'm glad to hear that master. (Renfield turns to notice several diminutive aliens peering in at the silently opened doorway. He excitedly waves them in...) Master? (again practically frothing with anticipation)

Dracula - Yes?

Renfield - Do you expect Lura might return someday?

Dracula - I don't know. Women are a fickle breed aren't they?

Renfield - (crunching sounds)

Author Bio

Richard Reich is the author of two vampire books and several short story collections dealing with horror, science fiction, mystery and unavoidably humor... He has a bachelor's degree from Davidson College, a school for the Liberal Arts and a medical doctorate from Fatima College in the Philippines. He's worked as a resident pathologist and cytotechnologist, but finds the relaxed pace of life as a writer more to his taste.

He can be found making his existence in St. Petersburg, Florida. Hobbies include the body pump style of aerobics, golf and cats.